WHEN FALCONS FLY

The Story of the World's First Olympic Gold Hockey Team

DAVID SQUARE

2nd Printing; October, 2007

www.poppyproductions.ca

Poppy Productions
Suite 203 - 1328 Marinaside Crescent
Vancouver, B.C. V6Z 3B3

Cover and text design by Karen Armstrong Graphic Design, Winnipeg

Printing by Premier Printing Ltd. Winnipeg, Manitoba, Canada

Cover photo courtesy of The Icelandic Canadian

Website design by Create Communications Inc.

Library and Archives Canada Cataloguing in Publication

Square, David, 1950-
When Falcons Fly: the story of the world's first Olympic gold hockey team /
David Square; Johanne Leach, editor.

ISBN 978-0-9782818-0-9

1. Winnipeg Falcons (Hockey team)–Fiction. I. Leach, Johanne, 1947- II. Title.

PS8637.Q37W44 2007   C813'.6   C2007-900845-3

Praise for David Square's *When Falcons Fly*

"I know with the magical thread woven amongst any good team, the Winnipeg Falcons are smiling down on this book recognizing their heroic feat."

Chris Oddleifson
Former captain, Vancouver Canucks

"It's a great story of courage and achievement and the good guys win in the end! A must read for anyone interested in Winnipeg's Icelandic history."

The Honourable Gary Filmon
Former premier of Manitoba

"Square's book emphasizes the racial discrimination that the Icelandic players had to overcome in order to play in a senior league."

Helen Norrie
Winnipeg Free Press

"I read *When Falcons Fly* in one sitting. I just couldn't put it down and went through withdrawal when the last page was turned. If you enjoy a good sports story you will love this book. I highly recommend it!"

Amazon.com

"David casts Frank Fredrickson as the main character in the novel, though all the other players are vividly portrayed as the team reassembles after the war and strives to win..."

David Jon Fuller
Logberg-Heimskringla

"It's a story of big dreams, big obstacles and big wins that incidentally portrays the coming-of-age of a generation."

Amazon.com

"Readers of all ages will be swept up into the energy of the team, while flying through each page, keeping pace with David Square's skillful play by play."

Shelley Harrison Rae
Wordlink

ACKNOWLEDGEMENTS

The author would like to thank the groups and individuals who contributed financial support to make the publication of this book possible:

Falcons Forever Committee
Manitoba Sports Hall of Fame and Museum
Dan Johnson
Norman Leach
Nick Logan
Jamie Tuckwell
Tim Dennehy
Jim Hedley

Thanks are also due to:

Fred Thordarson for writing and his daughter Shirley McCreedy for editing "The Romance of the Falcons," originally published in Canadian Sports and Outdoor Life and later in the 1996 and 2002 issues of the Icelandic Canadian.

Rick Brownlee and Andrea Reichert of the Manitoba Sports Hall of Fame and Museum for providing historical information about the Falcons.

Archives of Manitoba for access to the Manitoba Free Press articles about the Falcons.

Elizabeth Dafoe Library, University of Manitoba, including Special Collections and the Icelandic Collection and Reading Room.

The Logberg Heimskringla, North America's Icelandic weekly, the oldest ethnic periodical published in Canada since 1886.

The BC Sports Hall of Fame and Musem

Dr. John (Bud) and Alix Fredrickson

Frank Fredrickson Jr.

Brian Johannesson

Audrey Fridfinnson

Connie Johannesson Appleby and Bill Appleby

Viola Halderson Perkins

Beverly Byron Doyle

Kathy Woodman Mikkelsen

Sara Leach

Steinthor Gudbjartsson, journalist, Morganbladid, Reykjavik, Iceland

David Lee, special sections editor, Winnipeg Free Press

Sigrid Johnson

Ann Barling, former features editor, The Vancouver Sun

John Pawlyk

Joyce Statton

Fred Hume, sports historian, University of British Columbia athletics

Prof. Morris Mott, chair, history department, Brandon University

Leona Trainer, Transatlantic Literary Agency Inc.

Chris Hunter, a young man who read the first four chapters and said: "When is the book going to be published? I can't wait to read the rest."

With all my love to:

Penny and Bryn
&
Johanne and Norm, Sara and Duane,
Heather and Doug

"All my life I have taken care of falcons, and I will tell you
this. The closer to heaven they rise, the happier they get.
They understand that when they go very high something
changes in the world and in them. I have seen them, a minute
speck that you can hardly keep in sight, twirling in the blue,
and I am convinced that this is what they live for."

The Kelty Patrick Dennehy Foundation

Kelty Patrick Dennehy
November 23, 1983 - March 2, 2001

"When Falcons Fly is a great story about people overcoming and believing they can make a difference, something our board believes our foundation can do. It's also about having a dream and believing in that dream. This is what our kids need today, to believe in themselves and have a vision and strive for that vision no matter what the obstacles."

Ginny Dennehy
Director,
Kelty Patrick Dennehy Foundation

He Shoots He Scores by Rod Charlesworth

The author, David Square, and the publisher, Poppy Productions, are contributing a share of the profits from the sale of this book to the Kelty Dennehy Foundation.

The Kelty Patrick Dennehy Foundation was founded by Ginny and Kerry Dennehy in memory of their beloved son Kelty Dennehy who was 17 years old when he took his own life. He was a sociable, well-rounded young man, an avid hockey player and golfer, an accomplished athlete and high school honor student, when suddenly he was overwhelmed by depression.

The foundation works to remove the stigma associated with depression by taking a leadership role in funding education, effective treatments and research. By doing this the foundation raises awareness of the magnitude of depression in young people and the devastating effect it has on individuals and society.

Please visit www.thekeltyfoundation.org for more information on depression, its stigma and what the foundation is doing to make changes and to improve the lives of young people living with depression.

www.thekeltyfoundation.org

This is a work of historical fiction. Although the novel is based on a true story, some of the names, characters, places and incidents are the product of the author's imagination and any resemblance to actual persons, living or dead, business establishments, events, or locales is entirely coincidental.

CHAPTER ONE

Winnipeg, 1909

"*F*rankie, I'm open, pass me the puck." Young Frank Fredrickson stole the puck from an opponent at center ice and looked up to see his teammate Slim Halderson skating fast along the right wing. With a smooth sweep of his stick, Frank fed the puck up the ice to the right-winger. The pass was slightly ahead of Slim, but the gangly forward stretched to pick up the puck with the tip of his stick. He carried it into the corner, turning his back on a charging defenseman who slammed the shaft of his stick across Slim's shoulder-blades to force him off the puck.

"We agreed no rough stuff!" yelled Slim.

"Just a little payback, Goolie. That was an illegal forward pass," said the porcine defenseman. He slashed Slim's ankle with his stick.

Slim recovered his balance, regained control of the puck, and centered it in front of the goal where Frank had skated into position. The powerful center made no mistake. Without stopping the black disc, he swung his stick and fired it between the goalie's legs. A cheer went up from a small group of onlookers, mostly young women, who had gathered to watch the Saturday afternoon game between the Icelanders and the Anglophones on the frozen Assiniboine River.

Frank had learned early in life that the river was a boundary that divided Little Iceland on its north side from the Anglophone community on its south. The Anglophones or Wasps lived in a well-to-do section of the city with its epicenter at the intersection of River Avenue and Osborne Street. The Wasps, mainly of English and Scottish descent, owned the most luxurious houses that were built on the largest and most coveted lots on River Avenue, Roslyn Road and, especially,

Wellington Crescent. The Wasps composed the city's elite: affluent businessmen, lawyers, doctors, and politicians.

Most of the Icelanders lived in small single-storey houses or overcrowded duplexes and tenements in a poor part of the city, the west end, known as Little Iceland. The center of Little Iceland was the corner of Victor Street and Sargent Avenue; the latter was known as Goolie Crescent. The Icelanders' modest homes were packed with grandparents, parents, and children living together, sometimes in a single room heated by a wood stove and lit by a coal oil lamp. Yet, despite hardship, poverty and discrimination, the Icelandic community continued to grow.

Frank intercepted a pass and flipped the puck to Mike Goodman on left wing. At stake in today's contest was supremacy over the rink at the foot of Kennedy Street, near the Osborne Bridge. The losers of the game would have to clear the rink of snow for the rest of the winter. It was an onerous task that took many hours with shovels and long wood boards with handles, pushed along the ice like snowplows by the skaters.

Both teams played hard and fast. The Anglophones used their bodies and sticks to make up for their mediocre skating skills. Wally Byron, the Icelanders' goalie, had to get rid of the puck as soon as he made a save; otherwise, he'd be knocked to the ice by the charging Anglophones. No one wanted to lose this game. Aside from the benefit of not clearing snow, a win for the Wasps would prove their superiority over the Icelanders in all matters, including sports; a win for the Icelanders would boost their image in their own eyes, as well as the image of the entire settlement of Little Iceland. With the score tied at seven goals apiece and the sun falling toward the horizon, the pace of the game became frenetic. Soon it would be too dark to play, and a tie was not acceptable to either team.

Working to get out of his end, the Icelanders' defenseman, diminutive Bobby Benson, got control of the puck in the corner and ragged it up the right wing to Slim, who was about halfway down the ice. Slim received the puck and covered the distance to the opposition's goal in a few strides. As he prepared to shoot, the rover for the Anglophones charged across the ice, slashing Slim in the throat with his stick. Slim fell gasping to the ice. As he struggled to breathe, there were angry protests from the Icelanders who gathered around Slim. Frank spoke to his friend and helped him up while Bobby picked up Slim's stick and shook it at the Anglophone players.

"We get a penalty shot for unfair play!" he yelled.

"What's the matter, Goolie?" said the boy who had hooked Slim. "Can't take a little rough stuff? Maybe you're chicken? Bruukkk, brukk brukk!"

"We can take plenty," said Frank. He turned to face the Anglophone player. His name was Huck Woodman. He lived in a house with servants on River Avenue. It was surrounded by a wrought iron fence; the entranceway had a large gate embellished with a "W" for Woodman. His father was an architect, as well as a civil engineer with the CPR in Winnipeg. It was said Huck was wild and rebellious and had a chip on his shoulder.

"Okay, Frankie boy, why don't we settle this with our fists?" said Huck. "If I win, you lose the game. If you win, we lose."

"Big words from a Wasp," said Frank. "What does a rich boy know about fighting?"

"You'll find out, Goolie."

The two boys glared at each other, sizing each other up. Although Huck was two inches taller, he was less sturdily built than Frank, who had developed broad shoulders and big arms from doing chores at home. Frank had the blue eyes of his forebears, but he was stocky, not tall, and his hair was brown, not blond.

"Let it go, Frankie," said Slim. He held a tattered scarf to a bleeding gash just below his prominent Adam's apple. "You know what our parents said about fighting the Wasps."

Frank knew that Slim was right. He'd get a lecture from his father if he came home with a black eye. It was considered bad form among the Icelanders to become involved in a fist fight. Moreover, their Lutheran religion taught them that bravado and aggression were egregious sins. He stared hard at Huck and then turned to skate away.

"Look! The Goolies are going to forfeit the game because they're chicken," cried the fat, redheaded defenseman. "What's the matter, Goolies? Going to run home to your mommies?"

The entire Anglophone team took up the taunt.

Frank turned to face Huck and the rest of the Wasps.

"Okay, you win. We're not forfeiting."

"Does that mean you're going to fight?" said Huck.

"Sure I'm going to fight."

Slim put a hand on Frank's arm.

"Don't do it, Frankie."

But Frank shrugged it off and skated toward Huck. Both teams formed a circle around the two opponents. There were cries of encouragement from both sides.

"Show him your stuff, Huck," cried the red-haired defenseman.

"Keep your right up, Frank," yelled Bobby.

Slim remained silent as the two fighters held up their fists and approached each other. Although Frank was strong and athletic, he didn't know much about boxing. He could throw a left hook and, given the chance, let loose a powerful straight right, but he had no training in the art of pugilism. Huck, on the other hand, had won the boxing trophy at school two years running. He trained three times a week at a private gym because a well-rounded English gentleman was expected to be proficient in all areas of endeavor, whether scholastic or athletic. And next to hockey, pugilism was the most revered sport among the British gentry in Winnipeg.

Frank opened with a series of left jabs that were easily parried by Huck who countered with a left jab of his own. The innocent looking punch sounded like a ball peen hammer hitting hardwood when it exploded on Frank's cheekbone. Infuriated by the pain, Frank let fly with a straight right that Huck slipped away from, unleashing a five-punch combination that knocked his opponent to the ice. Frank got back up and charged Huck. The boxer backed away, landing punches until Frank fell to the ice again.

"That a boy, Huck," cried the redhead. "Show the dirty Goolie who's best."

"Come on, Frank, you can take him," said Bobby. Slim looked concerned.

Frank got back up. He felt fear as he faced his opponent. The Wasp, he thought, hits hard.

This time Frank approached warily, as a matador approaches a bull. He lowered his right fist, bent his knees, and let go with a right uppercut that would have broken Huck's ribs if the boxer hadn't blocked it with his forearm. Caught off balance, Frank tried to move away from his opponent. Huck took advantage by letting fly with a flurry of punches too fast and too numerous to count. Frank dropped to the ice like a person shot by a dozen pistols.

"That's my man, Huck!" screamed Fat Mac Jr., the pudgy defenseman. "You've killed the bloody Goolie."

There was some cheering from the rest of the Anglophones, but it lacked enthusiasm. Most of their faces looked tight and pale in the waning afternoon sunlight.

Slim and Bobby skated to Frank's side, tried to help him to his feet. He waved them off, somehow got back up to face his enemy once more.

"Give it up, Frankie," said Huck. "You'll never beat me."

"Sure I'll beat you, rich boy. Just give me time," slurred Frank, as he tried to focus. His face was bloated. Both eyes were shut. His nose and lips were bleeding. Blood oozed from cuts to his face and forehead.

Slim spoke to his older friend.

"C'mon, Frankie," he said, "let's get out of here."

"We're not forfeiting. We're not losing," said Frank, pushing Slim away. He staggered toward Huck, who had lowered his fists and refused to fight. But Frank kept coming. He landed a straight right to Huck's nose, causing it to gush blood. Maddened, Huck retaliated with a series of combination punches that hit their marks with brutal efficiency. A groan arose from both sides as Frank collapsed on the ice.

Huck stared at his beaten opponent. Frank's face and hands looked like butchered meat. His threadbare hockey sweater was covered with snot and blood.

Huck's anger left him.

"You've had enough, Frank."

Frank looked up at his vanquisher through pinched eyes. His head ached and his upper body felt as if it had been pounded by framing hammers. He spat blood on the ice.

"I don't want your sympathy, Wasp. Get away from me."

"You Goolies don't know how to quit, do you?" said Huck.

"That's right. We never quit. Quit is not in our Goolie vocabulary."

To the horror of all, except the redheaded defenseman, Frank began to get up off the ice.

"C'mon, Wasp," he said, unable to stand tall on his skates. "Let's have another go."

For the first time that day, Huck felt fear. How could he defeat an opponent who refused to be beaten? He also felt respect. Most rivals would have stayed down after the first volley of punches. But not the Goolie. He kept getting up. Where, he wondered, had his heart been forged? Huck knew he would never defeat Frank. It was a lesson that would change his life.

He turned and skated away.

"C'mon, it's almost dark," he said to his teammates. "Let's go home. This game is a draw."

Frank stood on shaking knees with his back to the Anglophones as they followed Huck off the ice. Frank did not fall again and refused to move until they had all left.

Fat Mac Jr., unsatisfied with the outcome of the fight, slipped back on the rink and skated full at Frank. The redhead held his stick crosswise in front of him. He drove the shaft into Frank's lower back near the kidneys. The loud collision and the scream of pain caused all the boys to turn and look. They saw Frank lying on the ice, blood leaked from his mouth onto the white surface.

"There you go Goolie, that's one from the MacPherson family. We don't abide Icelanders in our city."

The redhead turned to rejoin his teammates.

"What did you do that for, Fat Mac?" Huck said to him. "That guy has more balls than you'll ever own."

"He's nothin' but a dumb Goolie. My dad says they're nothin' but trash."

*S*lim and Bobby knelt beside Frank.

"That bastard MacPherson tried to kill you," said Slim.

"Don't swear, Slim," mouthed Frank.

"I can't help swearing, Frankie. That MacPherson is a coward."

"Don't you swear, Slim! If you swear, you aren't any better than they are."

"I'll swear if I like. I'm mad as hell about what they did. Aren't you?"

"Sure I'm mad." Frank began to raise himself on hands and knees. "But I'm not going to curse about it."

"Well then, I'll curse for both of us," said Slim. He circled his friend's waist with his arm to get him to a standing position.

Big Konnie Johannesson, who played defense for the Icelanders, also slipped an arm around Frank. Mike Goodman, the speedy left-winger, recovered Frank's stick, while Wally removed his goalie pads, layers of Eaton's catalogues tied around his shins.

Konnie exerted all his strength to haul Frank up the steep north bank of the Assiniboine River. Slim was a few years younger than some of the others and had not yet developed their strength and endurance. He was more a hindrance than a help to Konnie.

"Slim," Konnie said. "Let go of Frank. I can't carry both of you up this bank."

Slim let go with reluctance. Frank was like a big brother to him, something of a hero. Whatever Frank did, Slim did, too. If Frank affected a swagger when the neighborhood girls were watching, Slim would copy him. If Frank sneaked into a hockey game at the Auditorium Rink, Slim was not far behind. If Frank stole some chewing tobacco from his father's pouch, Slim would steal some smoking tobacco and cigarette papers from his father's stash, hidden in a cigar box in the basement.

Although Slim had older brothers, he remained in awe of Frank. Frank seemed to move through life with grace and self-assurance and absolute authority, as if he never had a doubt about who he was or where he was going. If he had any blemishes, they weren't apparent to Slim or any of the other boys who were drawn to him. He brooks no blemish in himself, thought Slim, recalling an Icelandic saying.

Slim thought about what other people said of Frank.

"Young Frank is a man of destiny," Rev. Bjarnason of the First Lutheran Church was fond of saying. "His destiny is in the field of music. A violin virtuoso, I think. What do you think, Frank?"

"Well, sir, I'd like to be a musician, but I don't know if I've got the talent to be a virtuoso."

"Nonsense! Of course you've got the talent. Inspiration is one small ingredient in a virtuoso. What's the other?"

"Well, sir, as you've mentioned before in this class, the other's perspiration," said Frank.

"Right you are, young sir! Perspiration is the stuff of genius. Without sweat you have nothing. You can have all the talent in the world, but without some good old elbow grease your natural gifts remain as flat as a wind-row in wet weather. Do you agree, Mr. Fredrickson?"

"I suppose so, sir."

"Don't suppose, Mr. Fredrickson. Get out in the world and kick some arse!"

The Sunday school class had broken into laughter. Rev. Bjarnason was capable of making outrageous remarks, to the delight of his students.

At the foot of Kennedy Street, Slim helped Konnie hoist Frank the last few yards up the grade to level ground.

"How are you, Frankie?"

"I feel like I've been beaten up by Jack Johnson," said Frank, unable to stand alone without the aid of his companions.

"Who's Jack Johnson?" asked Slim.

"The world heavyweight boxing champion, you dope," said Mike Goodman.

The legislative building, Government House and Fort Osborne barracks were illuminated to the west as the group moved along Kennedy Street. To the east, the teammates could see the lights of Kelly House, a mansion with classical pillars outside.

"Do you think old man Kelly will go to jail for stealing the materials from the Children's Hospital Fund to build that place?" asked Slim.

"He'll never see the inside of a cell," said Chris Fridfinnson. He played left wing, sometimes rover, and was always good for goals.

"How would you know, Friddy? You got an inside line to the city's bigwigs?" asked Bobby. He was nicknamed the Jumping Jack for his ability to leap on the back of an opponent, slowing him until he could be back checked by the rover or the returning forwards.

"As a matter of fact I do have an inside source," said Fridfinnson.

"Sure you do. Who is it? That gossip Mrs. Olafson who smokes rollies at the Hong Sing laundry?"

"Bugger you, Bobby. You've probably got a bat-on for the old girl," said Friddy, punching his friend in the shoulder.

"At least I've got one," said Bobby. He retaliated by kneeing his teammate in the right thigh and yelling "paralyzer!"

"Damn you, Benson, that hurt," said Fridfinnson, holding his thigh with both hands as he hobbled after his quick opponent. "I'm going to twist your arm off when I catch you."

The other boys watched Fridfinnson, who was leaner, taller, and more awkward, chase his antagonist down the block. The bickering between the two was usually a source of amusement to the team, but on this occasion it raised only faint smiles.

Wally, the most serious of the group, contemplated the Kelly mansion as the group drew near to it.

"It is a beautiful home. I think I could be persuaded to spend a little time in it. How about you Frank?"

"I wouldn't need any persuading," said Frank, beginning to walk on his own. "Just give me the keys and my violin and I'm ready."

"How about you, Goodman? You want to move in?"

"What a question!" said Goodman. "I'd give up speed skating to spend one night in that fancy shack."

"You'd never," said Slim.

"Just watch me," said Goodman. He pretended to speed skate toward the big house with sweeping motions of his powerful arms and legs.

All the boys except Slim laughed at his performance.

Slim stared at the mansion. The crescent-shaped concrete walk was illuminated by electric lamps, to Slim's mind a needless waste of money. The multi-gabled roof was shingled with clay tiles; the overhang was held aloft by towering white columns on stone bases. Every window in the house, including the arched entranceway, blazed with light. Slim could only wonder how much it cost to light such a house, let alone heat it in a Winnipeg winter.

"I hope old man Kelly goes to jail," said Slim. "No one should live in a place like that when other folks are freezing and starving."

"Spoken like a true Bolshie," said Goodman, pretending to skate circles around the boys.

"I'm no Bolshie," said Slim.

"Sure you are," said Goodman. "You're just too young to know it."

Slim looked at the rest of the group for support. Frank just shrugged, still too exhausted to support his friend. The rest of the boys looked away.

"Well, maybe I am a Bolshie. I don't give a damn. All I know is you could heat every house on Goolie Crescent with half the energy that pretentious shack uses."

"Pretentious. Nice word. You've got a well-developed social conscience and a vocabulary to match. You've gotta be a Bolshie, just like that Woodsworth fella," said Goodman.

"Knock it off, Mike," said Frank.

Goodman looked at Frank and made a zipper movement across his lips.

"Not another word will exit this mouth."

Then Goodman made an unzipping movement across his lips.

"But just let me add that Friddy was right. Thomas Kelly Esquire will never see the inside of a jail cell."

"And why is that?" said Slim.

"Because Mr. Kelly is a member of the British establishment. He may not be a Wasp, but he's got enough money to buy his way into the right circles, don't you know," said Goodman, doffing his cap.

"All the more reason he should be in jail," said Slim.

At Portage Avenue, the boys turned and made their way along the thoroughfare. Streetcars clattered by filled with Saturday evening crowds on their way to bars on Main Street. Most of the businesses on Portage were shuttered for the evening. Help Wanted signs hung from many of the storefronts. At the bottom of each sign in bold lettering were the words: "Icelanders need not apply."

At Balmoral Street, the boys walked north until they reached Sargent Avenue, or Goolie Crescent as it was referred to by Icelanders and Wasps alike. Sargent Avenue was the center of Little Iceland. The houses and tenements were, for the most part, small and overcrowded. The men found work where they could, some with established merchants of British descent who hired them because they could pay the desperate Icelanders a lower wage. A few families who had arrived in Winnipeg with a little money had opened small businesses on Sargent. They were Sigurdson's electrical, Bjarnason's barber shop, Johanason's shoemakers and, incongruously, the Hong Sing laundry operated by Mr. and Mrs. Sun Lee.

Frank's home was a two-storey brown clapboard on Elgin Avenue. The modest dwelling had a well-maintained picket fence enclosing a patch of snow-covered front lawn.

Wood smoke from a brick chimney was blown horizontal by a stiff north wind that made the boys shiver as they tried to make Frank presentable before he entered his home. Slim used his ragged scarf to wipe some of the blood from his friend's lips and cheeks.

"Frankie, you look terrible. Your father is going to whup tar out of you."

"No he won't. That's not his way. He'll give me a lecture and extra chores."

Just then, the boys heard a noise in the backyard. It was a pail being emptied.

Frank trembled.

"That's him in the backyard. He's flooding the skating rink. Now I'm really for it."

The boys watched Frank open the picket gate and limp up the sidewalk.

Inside, he was assaulted by the smell of boiled cabbage and fried whitefish. His mother was at the woodstove making the final preparations for dinner. Frank walked into the kitchen and sat down on a rough pine chair. He turned his head so only his profile was visible to his mother.

"Who's that?" she said, not looking around.

"It's me, Mother, Frank."

"Thank goodness you're home. I was just beginning to worry. You're late and your father is out back flooding the rink by himself. He's not pleased with you."

Frank tried to make himself comfortable on the chair.

"How was your day, Mother?"

"Are you feeling all right, Frank?"

"Yes. Why do you ask?"

"Because you've never asked me that question in your life before."

She turned to look at her son. She was a big-boned woman of medium height with braided blond hair, green eyes and a strong jaw line.

"Frank! Look at you. What happened?"

Frank attempted to turn his face further away from his mother.

"Nothing happened, just a little misunderstanding with a Wasp."

"A little misunderstanding. You look as if you've been beaten within an inch of your life."

She knelt before her son and examined his bruised face. Then she put her arms around his shoulders and began to sob.

"How many times have we told you to stay away from those people. Won't you ever learn?"

Frank looked away. He could hear his brother and sister upstairs washing up for dinner. Their voices were discernible through the thin plaster and lathe ceiling built of two-by-four joists, scrounged from a friendly Icelander who owned a small lumberyard.

The back door opened and Frank's father entered the kitchen. He was well over six feet tall, sinewy and lithe with a handlebar mustache.

His close-cropped hair was grey; his thin lips gave him a determined look. His eyes, a striking feature, could change color from pale blue to azure, depending on his mood. At this moment, they were pale and angry.

"What's going on here?"

There was a pause.

"Your son has been in another fight."

Mr. Fredrickson stepped closer to Frank.

"Stand up!"

Frank got painfully to his feet.

"Is this true? How many times have I warned you to keep away from the Anglophones?"

"Many times, sir."

"And yet you continue to disgrace yourself and your community. What is the matter with you, Frank?"

Frank looked his father in the eye.

"I didn't start the fight, sir."

"That's not the point. You could have refused to fight. We all have choices."

Frank continued to look his father in the eye.

"Sometimes we run out of choices, sir."

His father moved forward as if to strike him, then thought better of it.

"And this is your choice? To get yourself beaten almost to death."

Frank's mother intervened.

"Jon," she said to her husband. "We can discuss this later. Now your son needs medical attention. Send one of the children to fetch Rosa Gudmundsdottir."

"All right, Gudlaug," he said to his wife. "But this is not over."

He walked to the base of the stairs and called to his daughter.

"Sarah. Come quickly, please."

A young woman of 17 years of age appeared at the top of the stairway. If angels could manifest themselves, then Sarah was an angel—neighbors claimed her gentle soul emanated visible light, like the aurora borealis.

"Yes, father. What is it?" she asked.

"Run quickly and fetch Rosa Gudmundsdottir."

The slender, fragile girl moved down the stairs with grace, removed a worn coat and scarf from a closet, placed her brother's hockey toque over her golden hair, and pulled on boots that had belonged to her grandmother, who still lived in Iceland.

"What should I say to Rosa, Father?"

"Tell her Frank is sick and to please come immediately."

"Oh, not Frank! Where is he? What has happened?"

The girl moved around her father and ran into the kitchen.

Frank lifted his head from the kitchen table.

"Sarah," he said, extending an arm to her.

She burst into tears.

"Oh, Frank! What have they done to you now?"

Frank gathered her close to him. Although he was two years younger than his sister, he often felt like her older brother because she was so sweet and innocent. They shared a love of music that entwined their spirits and brought joy to them both.

"Don't worry gentle angel," said Frank. "I'll be fine."

Sarah ran her fingers over the numerous cuts and scrapes on her brother's face.

"You don't have to pretend to be brave for me, Frank," she said. "I know you better than you know yourself."

Frank smiled at her self-assurance. He might have managed a small laugh if his ribcage didn't hurt so badly. Sensing her brother's pain, Sarah slipped out of his arms and ran to the front door.

"I'll be back with Rosa," she said.

Frank's parents talked in the hallway.

"Jon," said Gudlaug. "Let's forget Frank's punishment for the time being. Jonas needs to be fed, and Sarah and Rosa will need to eat. Help your son upstairs to bed and I'll bring him some fish soup later."

"You are too soft on the boy, Gudlaug."

Nevertheless, he did as his wife bade and helped his son to his feet and walked him up the stairs to the second floor.

"Jonas," Jon called out, as he and Frank gained the landing. "Dinner is ready. Go downstairs immediately to help your mother set the table."

Jon carried his son the last few steps to the bedroom which Frank shared with his younger brother. He placed him gently on a lower bunk bed and covered him with a Hudson's Bay blanket.

"Thank you, Father," said Frank.

Just then the front door opened and Sarah entered followed by Rosa Gudmundsdottir. She was a kind, big-bosomed woman who had studied to be a nurse in Iceland, only to find that her credentials were not acceptable to the British medical establishment in Winnipeg. Before she could get a job in the city, she was required to rewrite most of her examinations to satisfy the local medical authorities. In the meantime, she ministered to the Icelandic community, asking only a small fee and a little food for her services.

"Where's the patient?" Rosa removed her coat, which had been neatly patched and mended.

From the kitchen, Mrs. Fredrickson called to Rosa: "Frank is upstairs in bed. Please go up."

As she made her way upstairs, the nurse berated all things British. "I don't know why we stay in this dreadful country. We should all move to the United States. It's a self-respecting country—not just the tail-hair of the British Bulldog! You're given a chance to prove yourself in America. I've told my husband we should leave at once. The poor man is killing himself in the service of a miserly English money-grubber."

When she entered Frank's room, her mood changed. She could tell from his irregular breathing that he was in pain. She reached out and placed a hand on his forehead.

"Where does it hurt, sweetheart?"

"My ribs mostly," said Frank. "I can't draw a full breath without pain."

Rosa removed the blanket and unbuttoned the front of Frank's undershirt. Her hands moved gently over his torso. He gave a gasp of pain when she touched the lower part of his ribcage on his left side. She explored the area thoroughly, while beads of sweat appeared on Frank's brow. When she was satisfied, she did up his shirt, replaced the blanket, and examined the cuts to his face.

"Well," she said, standing up. "You've got a cracked rib and a cut near your eye that needs stitches. How did this happen?"

"I had a disagreement with another fellow," said Frank.

"That other fellow wouldn't happen to be a Wasp?" asked Rosa.

"Why?"

"Because, no matter how hard you try, Frank, you'll never win against the establishment," said Rosa.

"Why do they hate us, Rosa?"

"They hate us because they fear us. Now try to relax while I stitch that cut near your eye."

Frank's mother appeared with a bowl of pickerel-cheek broth, a delicacy normally for holidays only.

"How is he, Rosa?" Gudlaug asked.

"He'll be okay. He's like the rest of us. He needs to get out of this miserable country before it kills us all."

Frank's father looked into the room after the women had left. He could see his son was having a difficult time falling asleep. Mr. Fredrickson approached the bed and stood near him.

"Tomorrow, I expect you to be up in time for morning chores and to attend church with the rest of the family."

"Yes, Father," said Frank.

CHAPTER FOUR

*T*o swing an eight-pound chopping maul was hard work, even when Frank felt at his best. This morning it was intolerable. The hickory shaft twisted in his bruised hands, causing the maul's cutting edge to strike the firewood at a skewed angle. As a result, poplar logs that normally split with a single stroke were taking five and six blows to crack open. Sometimes a punky one would absorb the tool's head like a sponge and Frank was forced to pound the maul through the rotten wood with the blows of a sledge hammer. At other times, a log with a twisted grain would reject the maul outright, kicking the tool back at his face. To make matters worse, a stubborn piece would fall off the chopping block; when he bent over to retrieve it the pain from his cracked rib would flare up, making him so dizzy and nauseated he had to lean on the tool's handle until the feeling passed. He was glad to hear his father call him to prepare for church.

When the family was washed, combed and dressed, Frank's mother and father ushered the little flock out of the house. The family walked to Bannatyne where they turned south for the trek to the First Lutheran Church at the corner of Sherbrook and Bannatyne.

Frank's father dropped back from the group and motioned for his son to do the same. Sarah, holding her brother's hand, did not want to be separated from Frank. She implored her father to let them walk together.

"Not just now, Sarah," said her father. "Frank and I have things to discuss."

Sarah, who knew her father's moods well, let go of her brother's hand and moved ahead to join the others. Frank and his father walked on in silence for a while. Mr. Fredrickson cleared his throat a number of times before he spoke.

"How old are you, son?"

"I'm 14, sir. And in a few months I'll be 15."

"Yes, exactly my point, and in a few years you will be old enough to fight for your country, and yet you continue to conduct yourself like a yahoo."

"A what, sir?"

"A yahoo, a savage—a person without discipline, direction, or principles. Surely, you've read Swift at school."

"Not yet, sir."

"Goodness! When I was your age, I'd read all the great novels. It's what Icelandic people do. We're the most literate people in the world. When your mother and I immigrated to Winnipeg, our families brought steamer trunks filled with books, not clothes or food, or bric-a-brac."

"Yes, sir." Frank rolled his eyes.

His father noticed the eye roll. "Stop saying 'yes sir'."

"Yes, sir," said Frank again, without thinking.

"Are you trying to get smart?" asked his father.

"No, sir. I mean, it's just that I don't know what you want me to say."

"I want you to tell me why you continue to conduct yourself like a yahoo despite repeated warnings to the contrary from myself and your mother."

They walked in silence again as Frank considered his answer. It was mid-December and large snowflakes had begun to fall from a white soft sky. Frank felt the flakes alight, melt, and cool the cuts and scrapes on his face. The large gash that Rosa had stitched the previous evening had swollen so that his vision was blurred in his left eye. He heard his father impatiently clear his throat.

"Well, the truth is," said Frank, "I don't go looking for trouble. In fact, I try to avoid it. But sometimes I think I'm destined to find it. I'd like to be a violin player and, in my spare time, an amateur hockey player, not a street fighter."

A horn honked as a family drove past in a new Model T. The car's driver just managed to avoid an oncoming streetcar that appeared out of the thickening snow.

"Destined is an interesting word," said his father. "We Icelandic immigrants have a destiny to preserve our culture, and, at the same time, to improve our lot in this new world. We will accomplish this by making peace and integrating our ways with those of the British, the Ukrainians, the Poles, the Jews; in short, all the cultures that make up this singular country. We will do nothing with our fists because violence breeds greater violence."

Frank considered his father's words. Ahead, he could see his sister and younger brother Jonas involved in a snowball fight. Frank's mother, who was between the two adversaries, was caught in a cross-fire and was pelted over and over by the white projectiles.

"How can we make peace, much less integrate, with people like the British who hate us because we look different and speak another language?"

"The British don't hate us, Frank. They're afraid of us."

"That's what Rosa said. But I don't understand. Why should they fear us?"

"Because in their hearts they know we are their equals. And they also know that some day we will take some of their power and wealth away from them. With good reason, the rich and the powerful fear strangers in their land."

Another streetcar appeared and disappeared. Its bell clanged non-stop to warn pedestrians and motorists alike.

"I guess I understand their fear. But I can't avoid confrontations with the Wasps. We play the same sports, and occasionally are at the same parties. Do I have to turn the other cheek every time I encounter a difficult situation?"

"My only advice is to stay away from the Wasps at all times," said his father.

Frank was upset by this unsatisfactory answer.

"But since The Vikings and the Icelandic Athletic Club united last year we have no real competition in hockey. How are The Falcons to become a good team if we never encounter any tough opposition? The Saturday games against the Wasps are our only way to improve our skills."

Now his father was upset.

"Damn it, Frank! Didn't I just tell you to stay away from them?"

Frank was surprised at his father's outburst. It was unusual for him to swear. His father must harbor a deep resentment of the Wasp community.

"What's wrong with playing shinny in your own backyard with your own kind?" asked his father.

"Well, nothing, exactly. It's good practice. We've learned to rag the puck, set up plays, back check and play defense, but now we need some outside competition," said Frank. "And you know the City League isn't going to give us a franchise. It's controlled by the MacPherson family, and everyone knows how they feel about us."

Mr. Fredrickson admitted his son had a point. Fat Mac MacPherson would give up scotch whiskey before he'd allow an Icelandic team to join the City League. Frank's father rubbed his fresh-shaven chin, seeking a whisker that had escaped the razor's edge. He continued to stalk his chin for several moments before he spoke.

"Can you keep a secret, Frank?"

"Sure."

"You promise not to tell anyone. This is between you and me."

"I won't tell."

"Okay. I don't want to get your hopes up, but I've been talking to Sam Johnson and Emil Goodman about setting up a Manitoba Independent League. We've already had positive responses from teams in Brandon and Kenora. We'd operate outside the City League and show MacPherson and his lot what hockey is all about."

"That's terrific news! Wait till I tell Slim."

Mr. Fredrickson stopped in mid-stride to look at his son.

"I thought you could keep a secret."

"Sure, sure I can, Father, but just how long do I have to keep it?"

"Not long. We hope to launch the new league after Christmas. But if we encounter negotiating problems, it may not become a reality until next year."

Suddenly Frank felt as if he were breathing pure oxygen. His aches and pains disappeared; his feet felt so light he seemed to glide across the surface of the fresh snow.

What an opportunity, he thought, to finally play hockey against some first-rate competition. Manitoba, he knew, was respected throughout Canada as a province that had produced many talented players. He recalled how one hand-picked Winnipeg senior squad had beaten some of the strongest teams that Montreal, Ottawa, Quebec City, and Toronto had to offer, much to the astonishment of the Easterners who thought they owned the game. He also knew that Manitobans were renowned for developing the wrist shot, the goalie stick, and were the first to protect their legs with thick pads, borrowed from the game of cricket. Frank longed for an opportunity to test himself and the rest of the Falcons against some of the best players in the game.

Mr. Fredrickson added a cautionary note.

"Don't get your hopes too high. There will be opposition to this proposal from some quarters. There is no guarantee this will happen. And we still haven't discussed your punishment for disobeying your mother and me."

In his excitement, Frank had forgotten about his fight with Huck Woodman.

"From now on," said his father, "you will practice your violin twice a day, complete your chores on time, never be late for dinner, and be polite to your sister's students when they come to the house for piano lessons."

"When will I have time for hockey?" asked Frank.

"You'll have to make time."

*T*he Gothic spire of the First Lutheran Church rose a hundred feet from its concrete base. The main entrance faced Sherbrook, where a Tyndall stone stairway led to oak doors framed with arched limestone. One storey above the entrance, three massive opalescent stained glass windows overlooked the street below.

Inside, the paneling and pews were constructed of the finest quarter-sawn oak; a pipe organ of mahogany and gleaming brass-plated pipes occupied most of the north end of the church. Although the instrument was magnificent and produced sounds of beauty, it was the subject of many heated discussions among the church elders, the parishioners, and Rev. Bjarnason himself. The enormous organ, after all, took up so much room there was no space left for an altar. This was rare in a Lutheran Church, where the altar was considered sacrosanct. As a result, many of the large congregation felt the instrument should be replaced with a less imposing one to allow Rev. Bjarnason sufficient area for a communion-table to conduct his services.

Frank and his sister were of the opinion that the organ should remain because it allowed them to explore the full range of their voices. Frank was a tenor and his sister was a soprano. There was nothing the two enjoyed more than to break into full song with the entire congregation while the sublime organ music reverberated around the vaulted church.

As the Fredricksons walked down the aisle to their accustomed pew, Frank looked for his friends.

"Frankie, psst, hey, Frankie," whispered Slim, who was sitting with his 10 brothers and sisters in a pew halfway down the aisle.

Frank nodded as he dared not speak openly to his friend inside the church. He noted that Konnie, Bobby, Friddy, Wally and Mike were seated with their families.

The service began with Hymn 329, *From Depths of Woe I Cry to Thee*, from The Handbook to the Lutheran Hymnal.

When the final notes of the hymn echoed in the church, Rev. Bjarnason stepped forward to address the congregation.

"On this holy Sunday, just a week before the birth of our Lord and Savior, Jesus Christ, I have asked two of our young parishioners to perform Hymn number 231, *We Now Implore God the Holy Ghost.*"

Konnie, who carried his violin, and Freda Johannsson stepped into the aisle and made their way to the front of the church. Freda was petite and pretty with dark, curly hair and brown eyes. She walked with the upright stance and assurance of a ballerina. Beside her, the big Falcons' defenseman looked ungainly, even though he moved with the grace of an athlete. When they stood side-by-side to begin their performance, the difference in their height and size was remarkable. Konnie was almost a head taller than Freda and outweighed her by 50 pounds. It looked as if the defenseman had brought his youngest sister, not his sweetheart, to perform with him.

Frank smiled as Konnie began to play the introduction to the hymn. He knew the defenseman would get ribbed by his teammates at the end of the service for performing with his girlfriend.

Freda began to sing in a clear, strong voice and Frank forgot everything and became lost in the words and music. Freda's voice became stronger and more beautiful as she began the second verse:

> *"Shine in our hearts, O most precious Light,*
> *That we Jesus Christ may know aright,*
> *Clinging to our Savior, whose blood has bought us.*
> *Who again to our homeland hath brought us."*

Frank marveled at the depth of feeling in Freda's voice and the mastery of the violin by Konnie: he was a skilful technician, but, more than that, when he accompanied his sweetheart he seemed to wring passion and pathos out of his instrument, qualities missing when he played alone. It was the same for Freda. When Konnie accompanied her, her singing was sublime; without him it was good, but not brilliant.

Konnie and Freda finished the hymn, bowed and made their way back to their respective seats with their families. The looks that passed between the two young people as they sat down were full of happiness and joy. Perhaps, thought Frank, playing an instrument for a woman wasn't so unmanly after all. He looked over at his sister and saw she was in tears.

While Rev. Bjarnason put the notes for his sermon in order, Frank wondered if a hockey team could play with the spiritual unity displayed by Konnie and Freda. Together, as a duet, they were indomitable, yet split apart, as soloists, they were more vulnerable, less strong. They needed each other to perform at their very best. What could the Falcons, he mused, learn from the couple's example? To play as a team, not just as a squad of individuals with no allegiance to their teammates; an unselfish group bound together by faith in each other, and a common goal of being the best hockey team possible. His thoughts were interrupted by Rev. Bjarnason beginning his sermon.

"This morning I will begin with a passage by Martin Luther on the meaning of faith. With Christmas nearly upon us, I feel it is appropriate:

"Faith is a living, bold trust in God's grace, so certain of God's favor that it would risk death a thousand times trusting in it. Such confidence and knowledge of God's grace makes you happy, joyful and bold in your relationship to God and all creatures. The Holy Spirit makes this happen through faith. Because of it, you freely, willingly, and joyfully do good to everyone, serve everyone, suffer all kinds of things, love and praise the God who has shown you such grace. Thus, it is just as impossible to separate faith and works as it is to separate heat and light from fire!"

Frank was intrigued by the sermon. It seemed to speak to him. If the Falcons had true faith, would God carry them to victory in their hockey games? If the team did good things for everyone, would God grant them his grace? But was God even interested in hockey or hockey players? Could hockey players be blessed as Konnie and Freda appeared to be blessed?

Frank was suddenly blown out of his reverie by the combined power of the organ, congregation, and choir singing *A Mighty Fortress is Our God*. He jumped to his feet and added his voice to the rest. As each verse was sung, he felt more and more sure of himself. Rev. Bjarnason often referred to him as a young man of destiny, a description which Frank had never believed. Yet today, for the first time in his life, Frank felt that he truly had a role to play in some great enterprise. He couldn't say what it was, but it was out there, just a little beyond his grasp, palpable yet, at the same time, transitory. If he could just reach out and grasp the thing.

"Frankie, Frankie! What's the matter? You day dreaming?" Slim stood next to Frank's pew. The service was over.

"Slim," said Frank, reaching out to his friend. "I just had the most amazing vision. We're going to be part of something really big, I can feel it."

"What are you talking about, Frankie? Who's going to be part of what?"

"You, me, Mike, Bobby, Friddy, Konnie, Wally, and…and someone else."

"What the heck are you talking about? Did Woodman loosen some of your screws?" asked Slim.

"No. I'm okay. In fact, I've never felt better. Let's go find the rest of the boys."

Frank turned to his sister and gave her a hug.

"I've got to go, Sis, I'll see you at home."

"Don't be late," she called after him.

Frank and Slim made their way to the back of the church where the rest of the boys waited for them. On the way, Frank overheard his father and Rev. Bjarnason involved in an intense conversation about Frank's potential as a violinist.

"Frank, you old slugger!" called out Mike.

"How are you, Frank?" asked Bobby.

"Welcome back," said Konnie, extending his hand. "I thought you'd expired."

"Good to see you, Frank," said Friddy. "Didn't you love Konnie's performance with the *little* woman he so cherishes?"

Wally, the most reserved member of the group, simply smiled at Frank.

"Thanks, boys," said Frank, who shook hands all around. "No more hockey brawls for me. Today you see a man with a new mission."

"What kind of mission?" asked Bobby. "Are you still trying to get a date with Beatrice Peterson?"

The teammates laughed. Beatrice, or Bea as she was commonly referred to, was a piano student of Frank's sister. Whenever Bea was in the Fredrickson household for a lesson, Frank would attempt to impress her with some athletic feat. His most recent stunt was to perform a one-arm handstand balanced on the top rung of a chair to show the young woman how strong he was. Bea, who was literate and musical, was unimpressed.

"What a ridiculous exhibitionist you are, Frank Fredrickson." Bea tossed her blond curls.

Frank's face had burned with shame as Bea left the house, closing the front door softly behind her. His sister had watched the episode from the small living room that also served as her piano studio.

"You're never going to win her that way," she said.

Frank's face turned redder when he realized Sarah had witnessed his clumsy attempt to woo Bea.

"Well, then, what do you suggest?" he asked.

"Play the violin for her. Women aren't attracted to athletic oafs."

The criticism annoyed Frank. If women didn't like athletes, why did they show up to watch hockey games? Wasn't hockey considered one of the manly sports along with cricket, rugby and lacrosse, all of which required tremendous physical strength, mental alertness, and moral discipline? If Bea didn't appreciate these characteristics in him, then she wasn't the one for him. The only problem was that whenever he saw the young woman, he felt compelled to win her interest. It was all right, he felt, for him and Sarah to sing and play music together because they were brother and sister. But somehow the idea of serenading Bea Peterson with his violin made Frank queasy. If his teammates found out, he'd be ribbed like Konnie. But Konnie was a big guy. He didn't need to prove himself to the world.

"Frankie!" called Slim. "Wake up. You're off in Wonderland again. Are you sure you're okay?"

"Yes."

Bea and a group of girls who sang in the choir walked past.

"Hey, Bea," called Bobby. "Don't you have a kind word for Frank? Look at the poor devil. He really took a beating for his team yesterday."

Bea turned to look at Frank.

"My goodness, Frank Fredrickson," she said. "I knew you were a show off, but I never thought you a hooligan and a ruffian, too."

Bobby couldn't contain himself.

"A hooligan and a ruffian!" he burst out laughing. "You've really made an impression on that young woman, Frank."

"Stow it, Bobby," said Frank.

Frank looked for support from the others, but he noticed even Slim had a smile on his face.

"What's so funny?" he demanded of his friend.

"Nothing." Slim collapsed in laughter with Bobby and the rest.

"Well, you can all stow it," said Frank.

"Don't get hot," said Slim, containing himself. "We're all friends and teammates. There's nothing wrong with sharing some laughter."

"Laughter at my expense," said Frank.

"Okay, okay. Settle down. You know what we're like. Sometimes we laugh at each other, but that's one of the reasons were friends." Slim put his hand on Frank's shoulder.

"You're right," said Frank. "I do get a little steamed whenever Bea shows up. I'm sorry boys."

Then he looked at Bobby.

"But I'm going to give this little jumping jack a paralyser, even if I've got a cracked rib."

The teammates hollered as they rushed out of the church to watch Frank attempt to run down Bobby who had a good lead and was gaining ground.

"I'll get you at the Monarchs game next Saturday," yelled Frank.

CHAPTER SIX

*T*he Monarchs game against the Victorias was sold out. Frank, Slim, and the rest of the gang patrolled the perimeter of the Auditorium Rink at the corner of Garry Street and York Avenue, hoping to find a way in. The main entrance was guarded by a bulldog-faced man named Mr. Legge who was hired by the rink's owner to eject gatecrashers. The boys discovered the fire exits were guarded by Legge's henchmen, mastiffs of equal ugliness and disposition.

"Damn, Frankie," said Slim. "We're not getting into this rink. They've even got the fire exits covered."

"Don't swear, Slim. How many times have I told you that?"

"Plenty. But I don't care," said Slim. "Are we getting into this game or not?"

Frank looked around. There was a trap door at the north side of the building. He took off his woolen mitts and tried to pry it open with his fingers, but the door was frozen in place.

"We need a lever," he said.

Mike looked about in an adjoining lot for a piece of wood.

"Try this," he said.

Frank took the piece of split railway tie from Mike, forced it under the trap door, and attempted to open it.

"I need a fulcrum," he said.

"What the hell's a fulcrum?" asked Slim.

Frank ignored his younger friend's language.

"Haven't you learned anything in school? Just get me a rock or something to put under the tie," he said.

Bobby found a small boulder that he rolled toward Frank.

"Will this do?"

"Fine," said Frank.

Slim, Wally and Konnie positioned the stone under the lever and, as Frank pushed down, the door sprang open. The boys stared into a large pit; a draft of cold air escaped from below.

"What's down there?" asked Konnie.

"It looks like a mountain of slush," said Slim.

"It's the scrapings from the rink," said Frank. "This is our way in."

He jumped into the pile and the others followed. To their left, high up on a concrete wall, there was an opening into which the rink's custodians shoveled slush between periods. Knee-deep in wet snow, the boys worked their way toward the hole. As they got closer, they could hear the roar of the crowd and the referee's bell inside the arena.

"Give me a boost," said Frank to Konnie.

The big defenseman put his hands together to hoist Frank up to the ledge of the opening. Frank slithered along an icy wood surface that led to a gap between rows of seats at the north end of the rink. From his vantage point, he could see four men with shovels waiting to clear the ice when time was called at the end of the first period. Frank lowered his arm to lift Konnie; then, together they helped the rest of the boys up onto the ledge. They huddled on the cold, slippery floor, looking up at the enormous Auditorium Rink which seated more than 2,000 spectators and had standing room for several hundred more.

"Hell of a crowd," said Slim.

"We can't see anything from here," said Frank. "Let's climb the stairs to the standing section."

"Someone will see us," said Wally.

"Don't worry. They're too excited to notice." Frank led the boys up a steep flight of stairs to the standing gallery.

No one in the boisterous crowd saw the boys reach the top of the landing and mingle with the rest of the spectators. The boys added their voices to the mob that urged the Monarchs to greater effort. "Speed, Monarchs, speed!" was the cry from the standing-room crowd. "Back check, Victorias, back check!" was the chant from well-to-do patrons with seats near center ice.

The great Monarchs' rover, Steamer Maxwell, had just started one of his famous corkscrew charges up the ice. He wasn't a big man, but he skated and handled the puck with such finesse that he was almost impossible to stop. Forwards Guinea Bawlf and Dick Wickson of the Victorias pursued Maxwell in vain, falling behind as Steamer turned on the speed. With rapid, elegant strides, he was soon in the scoring zone with only one defensive player to beat. Steamer feinted left and then shifted to the right, outmaneuvering a fat, red-haired defenseman who tripped on his own skates, falling flat on the ice. The Victorias' goalie, Cap Baker, took Steamer's hard wrist shot on the chest, but couldn't control the rebound. Anticipating this, the charging Maxwell regained the puck and fired it into a corner of the net.

The crowd around the boys went crazy. "Steamer, Steamer, Steamer!" arose from a host of voices.

The Victorias' fans were cowed, except for one man who had a seat near center ice. He hefted his bulk to a standing position, cupped his hands, and hollered at the defenseman who had been beaten by Maxwell.

"Get your useless lard ass up off the ice and do something. You're nothin' but a malingering bum!" He straightened the diamond pin in his cravat.

"Whatever you say, Daddy!"

Frank and Slim looked at each other.

"That rich fart is old man MacPherson," said Slim. "And that's his son, Fat Mac Jr., who cross checked you last Saturday during the game on the river."

"So it is," said Frank. He rubbed his jaw.

"How does Fat Mac Jr. get to play intermediate hockey? He's not good enough," said Slim.

"If your father is chairman of the City Hockey League and the richest man in town, you can play for whatever team you want," said Frank.

"That's not fair," said Slim.

"Grow up, Slim," said Frank. "I'm beginning to think you are a Bolshie."

The players lined up at center ice for a face-off. The referee rang his bell to indicate time in and the puck was dropped. Walter Gray, center for the Monarchs, won the draw and lifted the puck high in the air. It landed in the Victorias' corner where Fat Mac gained control and began to carry the puck up the ice. As he lumbered along the left wing, Steamer challenged him head on, neatly stealing the puck and passing it across ice to Gray, who began a charge of his own against the Victorias' defense. Incensed by the deft stick work of Steamer, Fat Mac lifted his stick and hooked the speedy rover around the neck, dragging him to the ice and opening a cut from Steamer's chin to his ear lobe. There was a cry of outrage from the Monarchs' supporters.

"Hey, ref, are you blind? That was a hooking penalty."

"That's more like it!" screamed MacPherson to his son. "Show them what you're made of."

It became evident as the game continued that the referee was doing his best to ignore the dirty tactics of Fat Mac. When Mac couldn't stop an opponent with a clean poke check, he knocked the legs from under the player with his stick. In the corners, he cross checked the wingers brutally or slashed at their ankles with the blade of his stick. The Monarchs became disheartened when no penalties were called. Time and again a charge up the ice by Steamer or Gray was broken up by Fat Mac who wielded his stick with impunity to fell his opponents. The Monarchs' fans were in a rage and screamed continuously at the ref to call a penalty. Even some of the Victorias' supporters were beginning to grumble about Fat Mac's tactics. The referee was booed from all parts of the rink when the bell sounded to end the first period.

"Hey, ref!" A fan rose from his seat near center ice. "How much did old MacPherson pay you to lose your eyesight?"

The referee's vision had not improved when the second period started. Steamer was taken out of the game with a broken ankle. Fat Mac had tripped the rover as he prepared to center the puck to Gray in front of the net.

"That's it for me," said Frank in disgust. "The only reason I came to this game was to watch Steamer perform. He's the best player in this city and now he's out of the game because of Fat Mac Jr."

The rest of the gang felt the same. Steamer Maxwell was their hero. They followed Frank down the stairs and along a hallway that led to the arena's main rotunda. The ticket booths were empty. The boys looked warily for Mr. Legge. A pretty girl with green eyes and a full red mouth sat at the entrance to the ladies' coat room.

"Hey, Frank," said Mike. "Get a look at her. If you can't get a date with Bea, maybe you can with this babe."

"Stow it, Goodman. I'm not in the mood."

Mike approached the girl and doffed his tweed cap.

"Excuse me, most beautiful mademoiselle. My name is Mike Goodman and one day I will be the North American speed skating champion."

The girl looked impressed.

"Get stuffed, Goodman," said Friddy. "You haven't even won a city championship yet."

Goodman turned to face his friends. "I didn't say *I am* the North American champion. I said *I will be*."

"You're full of yourself," said Friddy.

"Perhaps," said Mike. "But time will tell."

"More like the North American bull-shit champion," said Bobby.

Frank, Konnie and Wally leaned against a wall, laughing at the feud between Bobby, Mike and Friddy. No one noticed that Slim had left the group and approached the girl. He stood and stared at her until she turned crimson. Young Slim had no experience with girls. In fact, his older teammates' interest in females had always puzzled him, until now.

"You're, you're . . . you're beautiful."

"Thank you." She lowered her head so her hair covered her blushing face.

"I don't mean just beautiful," he stammered. "I mean more beautiful than any girl, anywhere."

"You're sweet," she said, still looking down.

"What's your name?" asked Slim.

"I'm not supposed to tell my name to boys," she said.

Just then a voice that sounded like the bark of a mean dog came from the coat room.

"Olive, get in here. Mrs. MacPherson's mink coat is missing. There's going to be hell to pay."

The girl jumped up and rushed into the room. The boys could hear Mr. Legge berating her about the lost garment.

"It's okay, Mr. Legge," Olive finally got to say. "Mrs. MacPherson asked me to hang it in a new place so it wouldn't rub up against what she called 'inferior furs'."

"Well, thank God for that," growled Mr. Legge. "We couldn't begin to repay Mrs. MacPherson for the loss of her mink. Now get back to your station."

Olive returned to her seat with tears in her eyes. That was enough for Slim. He rushed into the coat room and confronted the formidable Mr. Legge.

"Hey, Legge," said Slim. "You can't talk to her like that."

"Who the hell are you?" asked Mr. Legge, sniffing at Slim. "And how the hell did you get in here?"

"I don't have to tell you anything, dog face," retorted Slim. "Get out there and apologize to that beautiful girl."

"Apologize to that little slut! I don't think so," said Mr. Legge. "I know you. You're one of those Icelandic punks I've tossed out of here before."

Legge lunged at Slim with surprising speed and agility.

Slim avoided the oncoming charge by jumping to one side and kneeing Mr. Legge in the thigh. All the boys had crowded into the coat room.

"Did you see that? Slim gave him a paralyzer. Good for you, Slim. Give him another." Bobby cheered on his friend.

Although he was hobbled, the enraged Mr. Legge was not completely disabled. His eyes watered and his mouth drooled as he chased Slim between the racks of coats, snapping at the collar of the boy's ragged parka with his powerful hands. Frank, Wally, and Konnie held back while Slim and Mr. Legge tore up and down the room's aisles. Slim avoided the hefty man by sliding through narrow gaps between the racks or ducking under hanging coats. Friddy, Mike, and Bobby got involved in the action.

"Here doggie, doggie." Bobby ran up behind the perspiring Legge and flicked his finger on the back of the man's head. Mike and Friddy made barking noises to divert Legge's attention from Bobby.

"Arf, arf, over here, boy," they called. Legge looked rabid when he turned on them.

Coats were knocked off hangers and fell to the floor where they were trampled by dirty, slushy boots. Mrs. MacPherson's precious mink was the last to go. Legge made an attempt to catch it in mid-air by springing like a hound after a fox. He was too late. He landed on top of the coat as it hit the floor. He rolled around and around like a dog mangling a rug.

"My goodness!" said a woman's voice. "What in heaven's name are you doing in my mink coat, Mr. Legge?"

It was Mrs. MacPherson. She had decided to leave the game early and had come to collect her fur and her evening bag.

Mr. Legge looked up at her. He began to whimper like a puppy.

"Let's get out of here, boys. I can't afford more trouble. My father would kill me." Frank moved to the exit.

Slim waved to Olive.

"Goodbye, Olive. I hope we meet again."

"Goodbye, whatever your name is," she called after him. "I think you're very brave."

CHAPTER SEVEN

Winnipeg, September 1910

*F*rank's father was furious when his son announced his intention to quit school and get a job. Mr. Fredrickson argued that a good education was the most precious gift a man could acquire. He threatened to kick Frank out of the house if he abandoned his schooling. But Frank had decided he knew more than his teachers and refused to listen to his father. In truth, Frank was tired of living in poverty and was defeated by the discrimination he faced daily. The Independent Hockey League which held such promise for the Falcons had been quashed by the directors of the City Hockey League. They had no intention of allowing foreigners to disgrace the national sport by establishing a league of their own.

Frank walked into the law office of Laycock, Solmundson & Levine at 8:30 a.m. on a bright fall morning. The office was on the second floor of the Hammond Building at 63 Albert Street, near Bannatyne Avenue. It was a firm of mixed heritage which represented some of the wealthiest people in Winnipeg and some of the most indigent: *No client too rich, no client too poor* was the slogan the firm advertised in the Manitoba Free Press.

Sam Laycock was a kind, bandy-legged Englishman who lived for his weekends at his country house north of Winnipeg where he raised racehorses. Halson Solmundson was a first-generation Icelandic immigrant who had used his wits to become a senior member of the firm. Paul Levine was the son of Jews who had fled persecution in Russia to find a better life in Winnipeg's north end. The unlikely threesome made up one of the city's most unusual yet successful law practices.

Aside from their reputation as first-rate defense lawyers, the senior partners were known throughout the city for their love of hockey. Their firm had a mediocre team in the Lawyers' League, a highly competitive association. Winnipeg was crazy about hockey. Every business from Eaton's to the CPR had a team such as the Salesmen or the Engineers. There were even teams from particular streets such as Edwin Street or McDonald Street which played occasional games.

"Are you lost?" asked a female secretary as Frank approached her desk.

"I'm the new office boy," he said.

"How old are you?" she inquired.

"I'm 15," said Frank. He noted that she was in her early 20s and had lovely, long blond hair.

"I wasn't told you were coming," she said. "What's your name?"

"Frank Fredrickson."

"Oh, you're Icelandic. So am I. I'm Haldora Olson. Welcome to Laycock & Co."

She stood up and offered a manicured hand to Frank, who shook it.

"I'll inform Mr. Solmundson that you are here."

Frank looked about the room. Except for three offices along one wall, it was a one-room operation with desks manned by serious men who spoke into telephones or, in a few cases, interviewed clients in person. Frank noticed that most of the clients were attractive females, the kind his father would have politely referred to as ladies of the night. Winnipeg, he knew, had a reputation as the most sinful city in Canada.

The secretary returned and ushered Frank into Mr. Solmundson's office.

"Young Mr. Fredrickson, welcome to the company," said Halson Solmundson, standing up. He was a jolly, bald fellow in his late 40s with a bushy eyebrow that grew atop one eye to the other without interruption. The eyebrow undulated when he spoke.

"I can see from your resume that you're a hard worker, have a Grade 8 education, play the violin, and, let me see, you're also a hockey player! Well, you've come to the right place if you're a puck whacker. Are you any good?"

"I think I'm very good, sir," said Frank. "But I've given up hockey."

"Given up! I should think a young man would want to play the game 24 hours a day."

Frank looked about the sparse office before he answered.

"There's no respect to be had in the sport, sir."

"No respect! My God, Fredrickson, every sportsman in Winnipeg is mad about the game."

"In most parts of Winnipeg, yes. But not in my league."

"And what league would that be?" Solmundson's bushy eyebrow writhed like a caterpillar.

"The Icelandic Hockey League."

"Ah," said Solmundson. "The Winnipeg Falcons. The team that nobody wants."

"That's what they call us, sir."

Solmundson leaned back in his chair, tapped a pen on a blotter and thought.

"Well I believe in you Fredrickson because you're Icelandic and we have the hearts of Vikings. I'll make this job contingent on two things: you work hard at the office and you play hockey in the Lawyers' League for this firm. Believe me, if you're any good at hockey you'll get all the respect you can handle in this league. Now what position do you play?"

Frank was mesmerized by Solmundson's eyebrow. Before he could refuse the offer, Solmundson asked again: "What position do you play?"

"Center," Frank said.

"Capital, Fredrickson. Our team is shy one player and you're going to be the replacement. C'mon, let me introduce you to some of the boys."

Mr. Solmundson seemed to bounce out of his office, springing off the balls of his feet as if they were made of rubber. He climbed on a cluttered desk, kicked papers out of the way, and called the room to attention.

"Excuse me gentlemen, and ladies. I want to introduce our new office boy, Frank Fredrickson."

There was polite applause from the young lawyers. One of the well-rouged lady clients called out: "How old are you, sweetie? You're cute."

Frank blushed as everyone in the room laughed.

"Behave yourself, Minnie," scolded Mr. Solmundson.

"Young Fredrickson," he continued, "is a hard worker, a musician and, here's the best news—a hockey player!"

The office burst into applause. People who had shown little interest in Frank swarmed around him, clapped him on the back, and shook his hand.

"Glad to have you aboard, Fredrickson," said a short, ruddy-faced young man whose face was covered with stitches. He was the team's goalie, Benny Goodfellow. "We could use a talented new man. There's terrible fierce competition in the Lawyers' League."

After the initial enthusiasm, the members of the firm settled down to the daily routine, leaving Frank with little to do except empty waste baskets and shuffle documents between lawyers. When he looked at the clock it was only 8:45 a.m. At 9:05 a.m. he asked Haldora if the clock's mechanism was damaged as the instrument seemed to have stopped. The young woman took pity on the new office boy; she rummaged through a pile of papers on her desk, selecting one which she passed to Frank. "Take this brief across the street to Pickard, McGoey & Salad. It's a gorgeous day so take your time."

Frank fled the office with the document, taking the stairs three at a time until he reached the ground floor. He saw a boy about his own age entering the building by the door he was about to exit. The youth had short, neat brown hair combed smoothly against his scalp, wore a well-cut suit and walked with an assured gait. The two young men almost collided.

"Woodman," said Frank.

"Fredrickson! What the hell are you doing here?"

"I was about to ask you the same question," said Frank.

The two boys stood in the doorway, facing off, neither willing to move aside to let the other past.

At last Frank said: "I work here. I'm with Laycock & Co., the law office on the second floor."

Huck looked at him in disbelief.

"Sure you are," he said. "And I'm the Prince of Wales."

"I didn't say I was important," said Frank. "I just said I work at the law firm."

"What's your position, then?" asked Woodman.

"I, uh, do errands for Solly and the rest of his partners," replied Frank.

"Solly?" said Woodman.

"Mr. Solmundson and his colleagues," admitted Frank.

"I see," said Huck. "It appears we work for the same firm."

Frank was at a loss for words. He had not forgiven Woodman for the fight on the shinny rink on the Assiniboine River.

"I have nothing but respect for you," said Huck.

The boys moved aside to allow each other to pass. Woodman marched through the door and climbed the steps to the second floor two at a time.

Frank left the Hammond Building and cut across Albert Street to the Dingwall Building which housed the firm of Pickard, McGoey & Salad. He lingered on the sidewalk, feeling the September sun on his face and thinking about Huck Woodman. He knew little about the boy except that he was a first-rate hockey player who lived in a grand home in the city's rich Fort Rouge area. It was said that the Woodman family owned a considerable amount of real estate near Stonewall and had a large summer home at Whytewold on Lake Winnipeg. Frank wondered why Huck wasn't in school. Rich kids didn't need to work for a living. Or did they?

Frank entered the Dingwall Building, located Pickard & Co., and gave the brief to a tall, broad-shouldered man of about 25 years of age who was balding prematurely. The man identified himself as a lawyer and asked for which firm Frank worked. When Frank replied, the man threw back his head and laughed.

"Laycock & Co.! You've got the worst hockey team in the city. We're going to put you through the meat grinder. We've got the best team in the city."

"I don't think so," said Frank, angered by the man's boast.

"And who the hell are you, little man?" asked the giant as he stared down at Frank.

"I'm Frank Fredrickson. The new center for Laycock & Co."

"A Goolie. Beating you is going to be a pleasure."

"And who are you?" asked Frank.

"Bowden Braemar. The best center in the Lawyers' League."

"We'll see about that," said Frank. He turned and left the building.

Suddenly Frank was in a hurry to return to his job. He had some questions to ask Huck Woodman.

"Back so soon," said Haldora, as Frank came into the office.

"I want to talk to Huck Woodman," he said.

"You know each other, then?" asked Haldora.

"I suppose you could say that," said Frank.

He found Huck seated at a small desk pushed against a somber beige wall. He was proof-reading a letter Haldora had prepared for Mr. Levine.

"Back from your errand?" asked Huck.

Frank didn't respond. He was thinking about how to phrase his first question. He decided to ask it directly.

"Why are you working here, Woodman?"

"It's about hockey," Huck said. "In exchange for a couple of hours' work every Monday morning, I'm eligible to play for the firm's team. My father is a client here. He set it up with Mr. Laycock. They're both nuts about hockey and believe me this office team needs all the help it can get."

"What about school?" asked Frank.

"Oh, my father worked a deal with the principal so I can make up missed classes at home."

Frank was impressed. Woodman seemed okay.

"We'll be playing on the same team, then," said Frank.

"Believe me, Fredrickson, it will be a pleasure to have you on my side," said Huck.

Frank ignored the remark.

"Do you know a guy named Bowden Braemar?"

"That conceited lout, of course I know him. He played for the University of Manitoba and now he thinks he's the most gifted hockey player in the whole bloody country."

Their conversation was cut short by Mr. Laycock.

"I see you two lads are getting acquainted," he said with a strong English accent.

"We've played hockey against each other in the past," said Huck.

"Good show," said Laycock. "What do you think, Woodman? Do we have a promising player in young Fredrickson here?"

"More than promising, sir. Fredrickson is the best puck whacker I've ever played against. Laycock & Co. is about to establish a hockey dynasty."

"Brilliant." Laycock rubbed his hands together in anticipation of the season opener.

———————

The rest of the day lagged. There wasn't much for an office boy to do in the law firm. Haldora sent Frank on a few more deliveries to help pass the time. When 5:30 p.m. finally arrived, Frank was first out the door. He ran north on Albert Street in the wrong direction to his home. At Market Square, he realized his mistake, but by then it was too late. To get to King Street, he had to fight his way through a bickering crowd in Market Square, a gathering place where vendors and buyers haggled over everything from poultry to handmade furniture. Many of the sellers trekked to Market Square from rural areas to sell their goods to earn a few extra dollars.

"Hey, young man," an elderly farmer hailed Frank. "Why not take a fresh chicken home to your family?" In a wooden pen next to the Mennonite farmer, about 20 black-feathered birds with red peacombs strutted about, occasionally pecking at each other or peeking through the cage. The farmer opened a door at the side of the pen and grabbed at the birds. The chickens flapped their wings and ran about the enclosure, bumping into each other, clucking wildly. The farmer caught one around the legs, dragged it from the enclosure, and held it up for Frank's inspection.

"This is a fine young rooster," said the Mennonite, "tender as fish and much juicier."

Frank was tempted. Now that he was a working man he could afford to bring something special home for dinner. His mother would be proud of him.

"How much?" asked Frank. The Mennonite held up 10 fingers to indicate 10 cents.

"Too much," said Frank. "I'll give you eight." The man considered the offer.

"Okay, eight cents," he said. "But only because I can see that you are a fine young man." He dropped the bird into a jute sack, tied the top with sisal, and handed the squirming package to Frank.

Frank was pleased with himself as he pushed his way through the late afternoon throng. It was a fine, plump young rooster, but had he overpaid? His mother might have beaten the Mennonite down to five cents as she was a shrewd bargainer. Oh, well, he decided, it was his first major purchase as a family provider and it felt good.

A familiar voice caught his attention as he sprinted across King Street.

"Frankie, hey, Frankie."

It was Slim. Frank noticed his friend carried a pouch filled with pamphlets.

"Where have you been?" asked Slim. "I didn't see you at school today. You play hooky?"

"No," said Frank.

"Then what did you do?"

"I quit school to get a job," said Frank.

"Yeah, sure you did," said Slim, laughing. "As if your parents would let you."

"I'm serious," said Frank. "I know more than my teachers do, so why should I waste time in school?"

Slim stopped laughing. He stared at his friend with concern.

"You're not kidding. You did get a job, but I don't believe you really think you know more than your teachers."

"Of course I do, Slim. Why else get a job?"

Slim was taken aback. He knew his friend thought well of himself at times but this was too much. He thought about Frank's story.

"I believe one part of your story," he said finally.

"What part?" asked Frank.

"I believe you quit school to get a job," said Slim. "But I don't believe you're arrogant enough to think yourself better than your teachers."

The jute bag Frank carried began to move as the rooster attempted to escape.

"I do have a full-time job," admitted Frank. "My family is having a tough go of it. My father was really upset, but we might lose the house if I don't contribute. And Sarah's health is fragile, her medication is expensive, and my brother needs to be fed and clothed."

Slim held up his hand.

"It's okay, Frankie. You don't have to explain things to me. When my parents arrived here they had some money from my grandmother's estate in Iceland. But now that they have so many children to feed, everyone in the household has to help out."

Frank was shocked.

"I always thought your family was rather well off," he said.

"Not any more," said Slim. "What do you think I'm doing with these pamphlets? I get two cents if I can hand out the entire batch by nightfall."

Frank looked at the pamphlets. They were crude newsprint publications that trumpeted the cause of an organization called the Social Gospel. The feature article titled "Equality for All" was by J. S. Woodsworth. At the bottom of the page, Frank noticed a brief biography of the author: 'James Shaver Woodsworth is a Methodist minister, member of the Social Gospel reform group in the church, and a tireless worker for and supporter of the indigent of Winnipeg.'

"Gee, Slim," said Frank, teasing. "This looks like a Bolshevik publication."

"Woodsworth is no Bolshie," said Slim. "He's just a good guy who's trying to help folks like you and me."

"I guess. But I doubt that Mr. Woodsworth is going to win any friends with the ruling class in this city." Frank tucked one of the pamphlets under his arm.

"I've gotta get moving," he said to Slim. "Dinner is in the bag."

"What you got in there?"

"A young rooster. I bought it myself."

Slim looked enviously at the bag as Frank departed. Slim was called the human hockey stick by his friends for good reason. He was very tall for his age and his diet was very lean.

CHAPTER EIGHT

W. J. Billy Finlay fingered through photos that littered the top of his desk until he came across a shot of Frank Fredrickson, a young Icelandic player showing unusual ability in the Lawyers' League. Billy Finlay was the sports editor of the Manitoba Free Press. When he wasn't chewing on a Pathfinder cigar or lighting up a Philip Morris navy cut cigarette, Finlay pounded out sports stories on a Remington typewriter, using a two-finger hunt and peck technique. In the right bottom drawer of his walnut desk he kept a bottle of Canadian Club whiskey and a silver flask he carried in his vest pocket when he left the office. The walls of Finlay's small cubicle were covered with photographs of professional and amateur athletes, especially hockey players. Like most Manitobans, the sports editor just couldn't see enough of the game.

Finlay was stuck at the editor's desk that day. He looked about the newsroom for a reporter. It was a slow Saturday afternoon in November and most of the regular newsmen had already left.

"Hey, kid," Finlay yelled at a copy boy. "Get over here."

"Yes, Mr. Finlay. What can I do for you?" asked the boy.

"What's your name?"

"Alan, sir, Alan Pond."

"You wanna be a reporter, Pond?" asked Finlay, chomping a cigar.

"Oh, very much, sir," said Pond, a slender, pimple-faced youth.

"Okay," said Finlay. "Get down to the Amphitheatre and check out a hockey player for me. His name is Frank Fredrickson."

Finlay wrote some instructions on a piece of yellow copy paper and handed it to Pond.

"When you get to the Amphitheatre, look up this guy, Duke Pensky.

46

He owes me. He'll set you up with a phone in the press box so you can report back to me."

"Yes sir!" said Pond. "The Amphitheatre is a big-game rink. This Fredrickson fellow must be important."

Finlay rubbed his forehead which was black with newsprint ink.

"Not yet," said Finlay. "But I've got a good feeling about this kid. He plays in the Lawyers' League. It's not a bad league and they draw a good crowd. Now get out of here and report back to me. I want to know all about Fredrickson's hockey skills."

"Yes, sir."

Pond sprinted from the Manitoba Free Press building at the corner of Portage and Garry to the Amphitheatre on Osborne near the Assiniboine River. He was determined to make a good impression on his first assignment as a reporter.

The Amphitheatre had been built for horse shows in 1908. It was an imposing two-storey wood structure with a semi-circular roof with square turrets either side. By 1910, it had become the premier venue for pleasure skating and hockey in Winnipeg. So great was the demand for ice time that the building was kept open round-the-clock in winter to meet the demands of the city's sports enthusiasts.

Pond pushed his way through a throng at the entrance to find Finlay's contact, Duke Pensky. He was a dapper little fellow in a sharkskin suit who spoke in a whiskey voice.

"Jeez, kid," said Pensky, looking over Pond. "Billy must be desperate if he sent you. You're still wet behind the ears."

"I can assure you Mr. Pensky that I am a seasoned reporter."

"Sure you are kid," said Pensky. "C'mon upstairs and I'll get you set up. Have you ever been in a press booth before?"

"Of course."

Pensky led the way up an endless flight of stairs to the top of the building where a room with large windows overlooked the rink. Pond felt nauseated as he looked down at the ice surface which seemed hundreds of feet below. Pensky handed him a telephone and offered him a cigarette.

"Have a smoke, kid," said Pensky, yawning. "This could be a long afternoon."

Pond, who had never smoked before, took the cigarette and placed it between his lips. Pensky lit it with a gold-plated lighter.

"You may as well have a drink, too." Pensky held up a flask of whiskey.

"May as well," said Pond. "All reporters like a drink."

The whiskey hit Pond's stomach like hot coals in a cold boiler. The rush was immediate and gratifying. The cigarette tasted good, too. He was on his way to becoming a reporter. He placed a call to Finlay at the Free Press.

"Finlay, speaking."

"Billy," said Pond. "I'm all set up at the rink."

"Who's this?" asked Finlay.

"It's me, Pond, at the Amphitheatre. I'm ready to go."

"Did you refer to me as Billy?" asked Finlay.

Pond remembered he was a copy boy, not a reporter.

"I'm sorry. I meant to say, Mr. Finlay."

"That's better," said Finlay. "What's happened so far?"

"Well, nothing," said Pond. "I just got here."

Finlay angrily ground out his cigar butt in a brass ashtray.

"Call me back when there's some action," yelled Finlay into the phone. He felt like adding *you moron* as he broke the connection.

Perhaps, Pond hoped, the game would be exciting and he'd have something more solid for Finlay later. With the nicotine and whiskey working in his brain, he gazed down on the rink and discerned some tiny figures skating onto the ice. Both teams wore the LL emblem of the Lawyers' League on the front of their jerseys. Laycock and Co. was dressed in black with gold trim, while the opposition, Pickard, McGoey & Salad, was in white with red trim. From where Pond sat, the players appeared to be from about 15 to 45 years of age. Pond recognized a few players who had played with the University of Manitoba's senior team. Aside from those rare stars, the teams were composed of a ragtag conglomeration; all were proficient skaters but their abilities to carry the puck, stick handle and shoot on goal varied. It was easy to distinguish the excellent from the good and the mediocre from the poor. Frank Fredrickson, Pond could see, was exceptional. Even though he was one of the youngest men on the ice, it was evident that Fredrickson was a superb skater and packed a hard, accurate wrist shot.

Down on the ice, Frank was eager to impress his new teammates and to perform well in front of the cheering section of employees from Laycock & Co. Included in the group were the firm's three senior partners as well as the beautiful Haldora Olson and Minnie, the street walker who had teased Frank his first day at the office. Frank watched Mr. Solmundson exchange a few words with the senior partners of Pickard & Co. A sum was being wagered on the outcome of the game.

The teams prepared to face off at center ice. Frank, playing center, was against Bowden Braemar, the arrogant lawyer who'd been a center with the University of Manitoba. Frank was reassured to see Huck Woodman lined up as rover for Laycock & Co.

The bell rang to signal the start of the game and the referee dropped the puck. Fredrickson was surprised by the agility and ferocity of Braemar. The big man, who had a much longer reach than Frank's, swept the puck away and began a powerful rush down the ice. Woodman tried to poke check the puck off Braemar's stick, but the masterful center maintained control and charged the defense, splitting the two like bowling pins. The goalie, Benny Goodfellow, was the last man to beat. Braemar fired his shot. It was fast and hard. The puck would have caught the top corner of the net had not Goodfellow stuck his face in front of it at the last minute. He dropped to the ice to prevent a rebound. There was a gash over his right eye when he got to his feet, but he had control of the puck.

"Are you okay, Benny?" asked Woodman.

"Yeah, Huck, but I can't keep this up. You're going to have to find a way to stop that maniac."

The face-off was held in the scoring zone to the left of Goodfellow. This time Frank was prepared for Braemar's quick attack. When the puck was dropped, Frank managed to get control. He passed it back between his legs to Woodman who raced up the ice with the disc. At center, Woodman lifted the puck high in the air into the opponent's corner. His left-winger skated leisurely after the puck while a defenseman for Pickard & Co. scooped it up and began a rush of his own down the ice. Frank, in scoring position in front of the net, tried to back check the defenseman. He passed the puck across the ice to the fast moving

Braemar. There was no way to stop the speeding juggernaut. He plowed his way through the team, knocking Woodman off his feet along the way. As he loomed down on goal, Braemar made no mistake. His wrist shot was low and in the net before Goodfellow, screened by his own defenseman, had time to react.

A cheer went up from the supporters of Pickard & Co.

"Braemar, Braemar, Bowden's the man!"

Frank kept his head down as he prepared for the face-off at center ice against the triumphant Braemar who said: "Enjoying the game, Goolie?"

There were a few encouraging comments from the Laycock supporters such as "Let's settle down now, boys," or "Don't worry, there's lots of time left."

When the puck was dropped, Braemar won the draw with his superior reach and skated away from Frank with rapid strides. Woodman made a brilliant poke check to steal the puck from Braemar. This time, Huck lifted the puck into the right corner with the same result as before. His right-winger, no more inclined to mix it up in the corner than his counterpart, skated slowly after the black disc while a Pickard defenseman gathered it up and began a rush up the ice. When he reached the scoring zone, the defenseman unleashed a nasty shot a few inches from the ice that caromed off Goodfellow's ankle into the right corner of the rink. Pickard's winger fought a fierce battle with Laycock's defenseman for the puck. Winning the fight, the Pickard winger centered the puck to Braemar in front of the net. Confident in his ability, the big center teased Goodfellow with some deft stick handling before he backhanded the puck off the goalie's shoulder into the net. Goodfellow dropped to the ice holding his shoulder.

The reaction from the Pickard supporters was immediate and louder than before.

"Braemar, Braemar, Braemar," exulted the crowd.

"Bowden, Bowden!" screamed a gaggle of young women near center ice.

There was no reaction from the Laycock fans.

Thirty feet above the ice surface, the telephone rang in the press box. Pond picked it up.

"Yes," he said.

"Pond, is that you?"

"Yes," he said. "Who's this?"

"It's me, Finlay. What's happening?"

"Oh, Mr. Finlay. Well, nothing's exactly happening, sir."

"What does that mean?"

"Well, it's two nothing for Pickard & Co. and the game has just begun."

"Two zip!"said Finlay. "What's Fredrickson done?"

"Well, he's a fine skater sir, I can see that, but he's not getting much support from his wingers. The rover, Huck Woodman, is the only other decent player on the team, as far as I can tell. And the goalie Goodfellow is fearless."

"What's going on right now?" asked Finlay.

Pond looked down at the ice. Everything appeared a little blurry.

"It looks as if Laycock & Co. has called a time out. The team has gathered around the bench and Fredrickson seems to be in the thick of it. He's arguing with the coach about something. Wait a minute. They're coming back onto the ice. They're lining up for the face-off and—guess what, sir?"

"What?" said Finlay.

"They've moved Woodman to left wing."

"Great, phone me back when something exciting happens," said Finlay, breaking the connection.

The bell rang and the puck was dropped. Frank used all his strength and agility to wrest it away from the formidable Braemar. He flipped the disc over to the left wing where Woodman picked it up and carried it into the corner. There was a fight for control as the back checking winger for Pickard & Co. charged into the corner to challenge Woodman for the puck. Huck stood his ground, managing to dig the disc loose and center it to Frank who one-timed it at the goal. The puck hit the left post and deflected into the net behind the Pickard goalie.

Laycock & Co. went berserk. Haldora hugged Minnie while the three senior partners leapt to their feet congratulating each other. "I had nothing but faith in young Fredrickson." Solmundson kissed Levine on the forehead.

"Brilliant, young fellow." Laycock looked over at Mr. Pickard and smiled.

"That's only one goal," said Pickard. "I believe my team has two."

As the teams lined up for another face-off at center, Frank felt some of his natural confidence return. He had had time to assess the other team, to look for strong points and weaknesses. It was obvious that Pickard & Co. had a star in Braemar, but the rest of the players were mediocre, even though they fought hard. The key to this game, Frank decided, was to keep the puck away from Braemar as much as possible. To accomplish this, he'd have to win every face-off and rely on himself or Huck to move the puck up the ice. Goodfellow seemed an intrepid goalie. Hopefully, he'd keep them in the game with more daring saves.

The puck was dropped and Frank took control. Braemar, anticipating a pass to Woodman on the left wing, began to shift in that direction. Sensing this, Frank faked the pass and took off straight down the ice with the puck. For the first time in the game, he felt the joy of being in complete control of his body. His legs pumped hard and his strong arms swung back and forth as he picked up speed. He skated through the entire opposition, baffling the goalie at the last minute with a switch up that drew the hapless fellow out of the net as the puck sailed over his head into the top corner.

If Frank felt more confident after his second goal, so did Laycock & Co.

"Dynasty!" shouted the normally reserved Levine.

Laycock looked over at Pickard: "That's only two goals," said Pickard. "I believe my team also has two goals."

Up in the press booth, Pond was enthralled with the sudden turn in the game engineered by the teamwork of Fredrickson and Woodman. The boys kept the puck away from Braemar by quick passes between themselves or by faking passes which threw Braemar off stride, allowing the two forwards to move the puck into scoring position. When Braemar did get a shot on goal, Goodfellow managed to stop the puck, smothering the rebound before the center could get another chance.

Pond sipped whiskey and smoked cigarettes as he watched. There was something beautiful, he decided, about the combined play of Fredrickson and Woodman. It was as if they could read each other's minds. They performed an intricate dance on ice that resolved itself time and again in a goal by Fredrickson.

The phone rang in the press booth.

"Yesh," said Pond.

"Pond, is that you?"

"Yes, it shurtainly is. Who's this?"

"Who do you think it is?" said Finlay.

"Jush let me guess," said Pond. "It's Billy Finlay."

"Pond, are you drunk?"

"Yes, shirr," said Pond.

"Jeezzzus!" said Finlay. "Are you at least sober enough to tell me what's going on?"

"Oh, yesh," said Pond. "It's 13 to two in favour of one team."

"Which team?" asked Finlay.

"The team in black with the pretty gold piping, shurr."

"You mean Laycock & Co.?"

"Yesh, the very one."

"How did Fredrickson play?"

"Amazing, shurr, jus amazing."

"Listen, Pond, get yourself some strong coffee and get your ass back to the Free Press building. I want a play by play and you'd better deliver."

"Of coursh," said Pond.

Finlay turned to his typewriter, rubbed a pencil between his hands and began his story:

Goolie and Wasp Demolish Perennial Hockey Powerhouse
*Natural enemies unite to crush powerful
opposition in Lawyers' League*

A young Icelander and the son of a well-known Winnipeg businessman combined talents to rout the powerful team of Pickard, McGoey & Salad by a lopsided score of 13-2 at the Amphitheatre yesterday...

*T*he senior partners of Laycock & Co. were elated with the performance of Fredrickson and Woodman. After their initial victory against the team from Pickard & Co., Frank and Huck continued to rack up wins. By mid-December, Laycock & Co. had secured first place in the Lawyers' League and there were still two months left in the season. Fredrickson had contributed 60 goals, Woodman had tallied 50 assists as well as five goals of his own, while Goodfellow maintained a streak of eight straight shut outs. Never in commercial league history had one team exhibited such dominance. The team's pre-eminence had earned Laycock & Co. respect and, along with it, new business in Winnipeg, as well as a small fortune made on side bets with other senior partners.

A week before Christmas, Frank was summoned to Solmundson's office. Frank was surprised to see all three partners were in the room. They all looked serious, yet happy at the same time.

"Take a seat, young man." Laycock pulled up a chair for Frank.

Frank wasn't sure how to read their faces.

"There's no easy way to put this," said Laycock," so I'll come right out and say it. We've decided to fire you, son."

Frank was shaken and confused.

"Fire me! But why? I've been a hard worker and I've contributed to your hockey team, haven't I?"

"You've been an excellent employee," said Laycock. "And I cannot begin to estimate the glory you have brought this firm through your outstanding ability as a hockey player."

"It sounds as if you should be promoting me, not firing me," he said.

All three senior partners laughed.

"Yes," said Laycock. "Under normal circumstances we would be promoting you. But your circumstances are unusual, so we have agreed to fire you."

Frank shook his head. He didn't understand. Solmundson bounced up from behind his desk and approached the boy.

"Listen, Frank," he said. "You're wasting your time here. We want you to return to school and get an education. We also want you to play hockey with your old team, the Falcons. You're too intelligent and too talented to remain an office boy and a star in a commercial league for the rest of your life. We're releasing you, son, because we have great expectations for you."

Frank sat back in his chair subdued, and still uncertain.

"But I need this job to help my family," he protested.

The three partners looked at each other. It was Mr. Levine who spoke.

"We have arranged to pay you a monthly stipend so you can return to school. We spoke to your father—a very proud man—who refused to accept our offer at first. But when we explained it was the least we could do, that you had earned every cent, he relented as he too wants you to get an education. Go home young man and, please, never stop playing hockey."

Levine held out his hand to Frank. He stood up and shook it.

"What about the office team?" he asked. "I don't want to abandon it now."

"Don't worry, son," said Solmundson. "We're so far ahead that no one can catch us. And since you've been around, the boys have learned to play better hockey. We'll be fine."

"Will Huck continue to play for you?" asked Frank.

"He can, of course," said Solmundson. "But if you want some unsolicited advice, I'd offer him a position with the Falcons."

The idea of inviting a Wasp to play on an Icelandic squad seemed preposterous to Frank, especially a Wasp like Woodman who was a blue blood of the first order. Surely he'd never agree to join a motley team like the Falcons, a team that wore patched jerseys, none of which were the same color, and used layers of newspaper and Eaton's catalogues as shin pads.

The partners led Frank out of Solmundson's office to the main room where Haldora and the rest of the firm's employees had gathered round a large chocolate cake with the inscription: Good Luck Frank, Onwards and Upwards. The whole staff was in on the conspiracy, thought Frank.

Haldora handed him a knife and he cut a big piece for her. Next came Minnie, who had taken time from her job to attend, and of course another slice for Woodman; and large slices for the senior partners, and an extra big portion for the courageous Benny Goodfellow.

Frank's eyes began to water.

"I never imagined it would be so nice to be fired," he said, keeping his head down.

His friends laughed and gathered close to him. He hugged Haldora and then Minnie, and shook hands all around.

"Goodbye, Frank!"

Huck walked downstairs with him to the main floor.

He extended his hand. "All the best, Frank. It's been a pleasure to be your teammate."

Frank hesitated. This might be his last opportunity to speak privately with Woodman.

"How would you like to play for the Falcons, Huck?"

Frank expected Woodman to scoff or reject the offer outright.

"I'd love to."

"You're kidding," said Frank.

"I'm not kidding. Notify me of your next practice and I'll be there."

Frank left the building. The cold winter air felt fresh and good as it invaded his lungs.

CHAPTER TEN

*T*he Manitoba Independent League was finally launched in 1911. It had required hard work by a number of prominent Icelandic and rural businessmen to put the league together, including the efforts of Hebbie Axford, the young president of the Falcons. The Independent League comprised the Falcons as well as teams from Selkirk, Brandon and Kenora. The hockey hicks, as they were referred to by the establishment, played proficient hockey but were still considered inferior to City League teams. The suggestion of a championship match between the Independent League and the City League to determine the best hockey squad in Manitoba was met with derision by the smug businessmen who controlled sports in Winnipeg. The city's elite couldn't imagine a team of intelligent, disciplined British boys lowering themselves to compete against the offspring of immigrants and farmers.

After he left Laycock and Co., Frank spent most of his time catching up on school work and practicing his violin with his beloved sister, who accompanied him on the piano.

"That was a beautiful arpeggio, Frank," said Sarah.

Frank put aside his violin and sat down on the piano bench next to his sister.

"Thank you, Sarah."

He was shocked by how thin his sister had grown in a few months, her skin translucent, her wrist so tiny he could more than wrap his hand around it.

"You've been working too hard. You know what the doctor said about your health. It's fragile and you need as much rest as possible.

You don't want to come down with tuberculosis, do you?"

"Of course not, Frank. But I do wish to contribute to the family by giving music lessons."

"I know you do. But, please, just be a little easier on yourself."

Frank hugged his sister who felt skeletal in his embrace.

"I have a gift for you," she said.

She reached for a little jewelry box resting on a rough pine end table. Inside was a white pebble with a hole in the middle.

"It's a Gimli stone," she said. "I found it for you last summer on that crescent-shaped beach that sweeps into Lake Winnipeg. They say these one-holed stones are sacred and unique to that area."

Frank clasped the little stone in his hand.

"I'll carry this with me always," he said. "And as long as I have it, you'll be safe."

He hugged his sister again and she kissed him on the forehead.

At that moment, there was a knock at the front door and a commotion outside.

"Frankie, let's get this practice started," cried Slim. "It's freezing out here."

Slim and the gang had arrived for an evening practice on the rink behind Frank's house. It was a windy night and the temperature was 30 below zero.

"You can put your skates on in the mud porch," said Frank, opening the door and allowing the troop to invade the house. The boys marched though the kitchen to the back porch where wood benches had been built along the wall to accommodate skate changing.

Mr. Fredrickson entered the room as the boys laced up.

"I've got a surprise for you tonight, lads," he said. "I've enlisted the help of a new coach."

There was silence in the room. The boys weren't sure if Mr. Fredrickson was kidding.

"Who is he?" asked Slim.

"You'll find out soon enough," said Mr. Fredrickson.

The back door opened and Steamer Maxwell clomped into the room, shod in his skates, covered in frost, and angry that the boys were taking such a long time to get onto the ice.

"Move your asses," said Steamer. "The evening is wasting. If you want to be hockey players, you've gotta have discipline and spirit."

Maxwell was 20 years of age, only about five years older than most of the boys, but his voice packed authority and he was revered for his athletic abilities, which included hockey and baseball. The boys hurried to finish lacing their skates. Frank led the team onto the backyard rink where Steamer had set up an obstacle course of blocks of snow.

"Okay, gentlemen, starting with Fredrickson I want you to skate a zigzag course between those blocks as fast as you can," he said. "Do it without your sticks."

Frank started fast but a short way into the course he began to slow down; Steamer had placed the blocks closer together as the course progressed, making it difficult to maintain speed and weave between the obstacles at the same time.

"C'mon, Fredrickson," yelled Steamer. "My grandmother could out skate you."

Next in line was Goodman. He fared somewhat better than Frank as he was a speed skater who had learned to keep his balance while cutting tight corners. He was far and away the fastest man on the team.

A new player appeared on the ice while the boys skated through the course again.

"Who the hell are you?" demanded Steamer. "You're late and I don't abide latecomers."

Frank looked up and saw Huck Woodman moving toward him.

"Sorry, I'm late, Frank," said Huck. "I had a pile of homework to catch up on before I could leave the house."

"That's okay, you're here now," said Frank.

He turned to face his teammates.

"Let me introduce you to a new member of the Falcons. He's my friend and one heck of a fine hockey player," said Frank.

The boys glared at Huck Woodman.

Finally, Slim spoke up.

"Are you nuts, Frankie? That's the guy who nearly killed you. And he's a Wasp. No Wasp is going to play on a team of Icelanders."

Frank and Huck looked at the group.

"You're right about one thing, Slim," said Frank. "He's the guy who beat me up. But you're wrong about a Wasp not wanting to play for us. He's here isn't he?"

Woodman interjected: "There's nothing I'd rather do than play for the Falcons, if it's okay with you fellows."

Steamer Maxwell spoke up: "We're here to practice hockey, not to argue about who's on the team. If Fredrickson says Woodman is a good player, then he's okay by me. Any objections?"

There weren't any objections, although Slim slapped a shard of ice at Woodman's shins with his stick.

"Nice pair of cricket pads," said Slim. "How much did they cost?"

Before Huck could answer, Steamer had the boys lined up for another try at the obstacle course.

"This time I want each man to carry the puck and stick handle his way through the course. Let's show some hustle. You've got a game against Selkirk next weekend."

CHAPTER ELEVEN

*T*he Falcons practiced hard all week for their game against Selkirk. The Fishermen were a powerful team with some of the finest young hockey talent in the province. Bullet Joe Simpson, Harry Oliver and Crutchy Morrison were just a few of the stars who made up the squad. As the game was to be played in Selkirk, the formidable Fishermen would also have the advantage of a home team crowd, a fact not lost on Frank and the rest of the Falcons as they climbed aboard Canadian Pacific Railway Train Number Seven bound for the fishing villages north of Winnipeg.

The car the boys occupied was called the *Duchess of Clandeboye*. It had hard bench seats, cracked windows, and so little heat they could see their breath as the train pulled out of the CPR station on Higgins Avenue. Huck complained about the lack of heat to the conductor.

"I'm so sorry," said the scrawny Englishman whose name tag said Edwin Scourge, "but this is a third-class carriage. If you want comfort, next time purchase a first-class ticket."

"Geez, he's a grouch," said Slim, who'd already made a tour of the train. "You should see what the hoity-toity are eating in the first-class dining car: leg of lamb, roast potatoes, and cauliflower in a cream sauce. And that's just the first course."

"What do you care, Slim," said Goodman, tossing a bagged lunch at his friend. "You're a Bolshie. You don't eat bourgeois food."

"Maybe not," said Slim. "But just once I'd like to sit down in a dining car and eat my fill."

There wasn't any argument from the rest of the team. They all had a lean look.

"Excuse me, boys," said Woodman. "But I didn't bring a lunch. I assumed we'd eat in the dining car like the other passengers."

His teammates burst out laughing.

"Yeah, right," said Bobby. "As if they'd allow us into the dining car, even if we could afford the price of a meal."

Woodman stood up and left. The narrow walkway between the cars was full of blowing snow which sifted up from the rails, finding its way into every crevice in the gangway between cars.

The dining room, he discovered, was three cars forward. Just before it was a plush, first-class smoker filled with businessmen, most traveling to Gimli to purchase pickerel and whitefish for restaurants in Winnipeg and as far away as New York.

Woodman, dressed in a new tweed jacket, corduroys, and a gleaming pair of brown brogues, fit the dress code of the well-to-do who inhabited the first-class carriage. He was hailed by a school chum.

"Huck," called Charlie Gardner, a smiling youth with unkempt blond hair.

"Hello, Charlie," said Huck.

"What are you up to, Huck? On your way to Gimli with the rest of us? My father brought me so I could learn to buy fish for our restaurants in Winnipeg."

"I'm not headed to Gimli," said Huck. "I'm going to Selkirk with a hockey team I play for."

"What's the team's name?" asked Charlie.

"The Falcons."

"The team that nobody wants!" exclaimed Charlie. "Are you off your nut, Huck? They're Icelanders. You'll be banned from senior hockey in Winnipeg if you stick with that lot."

The train lurched as it began to gain speed.

"I don't give a damn if I'm banned," said Woodman. "I like these guys. And they're exceptional hockey players."

Charlie looked doubtful.

"I guess you know what you're doing," he conceded, then invited Huck to join him for lunch in the dining car.

"Sure," said Woodman, "as long as you don't mind eating with some of my teammates."

"Of course not," said Charlie, wearing his best poker face. "The more the merrier."

Huck returned with the Falcons. Frank wore an off-white cotton shirt that had been patched many times over; his clean but well-worn dungarees were held up by threadbare suspenders. Slim's pants, also held up by suspenders, were several inches too short, exposing his skinny ankles and a pair of boots with holes at the sides from which his toes protruded. Mike, whose family was a little better off than the other boys', was presentable in a new wool cardigan and black cotton trousers. The rest of the teammates were dressed like Frank and Slim, in clothes that had been patched and handed down so many times they had the look of jute sacks.

"Charlie," said Huck, "I want you to meet the Falcons."

"Well, well," said Charlie, extending his hand.

Huck led them forward to the dining car. The boys were overwhelmed by the tantalizing smells. The tables were covered with white linen, folded blue napkins, and silver flatware. Silver pots of tea and coffee graced each table, as did a selection of white and red wines.

Before the boys were seated, the grouchy conductor, Edwin Scourge, arrived.

"Excuse me, but I don't recall any of you, except for Mr. Gardner, of course, holding a first-class ticket. All of you please get out of my dining car at once, excepting Mr. Gardner, of course."

Huck stepped forward.

"Excuse me, sir, but I do in fact hold a first-class ticket," he said, removing a piece of paper from the pocket of his expensive tweed jacket. "And if you care to read it, there is a note from my father, John Woodman, saying that Huck Woodman, that would be myself, and any of his companions should be treated with the utmost respect and courtesy while traveling on the CPR."

Edwin Scourge was not a bright man, but the name John Woodman did hammer a bell in his mind. Wasn't Mr. John Woodman, he thought, the very same man who was a vice-president of the CPR—and this Huck Woodman was his son—impossible! Why would the son of such a notable Winnipegger be traveling with such a bunch of young rascals? Yet young Woodman was well-dressed and he obviously knew young Gardner, who came from an excellent family. This Huck Woodman must be the actual son of John Woodman Esq., vice-president of the CPR.

Mr. Scourge barked out an order.

"You, darkie!" he called. "Make sure a table is set for these young men and get them anything they want."

A black waiter appeared and winked at the boys.

"Well, gentlemen, why don't you get yourselves seated and I'll start you off with some hot vegetable barley soup, fresh-baked rolls, and tossed salad. The main course is leg of lamb with roast potatoes, creamed cauliflower, baby carrots, wild rice, and stuffed squash."

The boys sat at a long table that took up a good portion of the dining car. There were grumblings from other patrons who had their tables pushed into corners to accommodate the merry group.

"I propose a toast to Huck Woodman," said Slim. "You've turned out to be a fine fellow."

"What are you going to toast him with?" asked Frank.

"How about this," said Slim. He hoisted a bottle of wine from a gleaming ice bucket next to him.

"I'd be careful with that stuff," said Huck, who was an accomplished drinker; his family served wine at dinner and brandy afterwards.

The black waiter reappeared with a corkscrew.

"Mr. Scourge said to treat you gentlemen just as fine as can be and I intend to do it," he said. There was a twinkle in the black man's eye that suggested he was enjoying the meal as much as the boys.

"Okay," said Frank. "Let's have one toast to Huck and then we'll eat."

But after the first toast, Slim decided a second toast should be drunk to the Falcons. And then Goodman suggested a toast to the Selkirk Fishermen, who were all good lads. Bobby thought they should toast pretty girls, while Konnie wanted to lift his glass to the great sport of hockey. Finally Wally, normally subdued, proposed they all drink to life in general.

When the soup and salads arrived, Slim uncorked a fresh bottle of wine and proposed a toast to Olive, the girl he had met briefly at the Auditorium Rink.

"I think I've seen that girl in the west end," said Friddy. He had remained uncommonly silent until that point. "Her name is Olive McKay and her family lives somewhere around Goolie Crescent."

"How would you know that, Friddy?" asked Slim.

"Because I keep an eye on all the pretty girls," said Friddy. "In fact, if I'm thinking of the right girl, Olive is running in a beauty queen pageant next month at the community club."

As the wine flowed and the food was served, the boys became more and more boisterous. Many toasts to Olive the Beauty Queen were requested by Slim. By the time the train pulled into the Selkirk station the dining car was empty except for the ebullient group of hockey players.

"Are we here already?" asked Slim. "Seems like we just got on board."

 Frank leaned over to ask Huck a question.

"Do you really have a note from your father in your pocket?"

"Of course not." Huck dropped some money on the table, leaving a generous tip for the waiter.

A rowdy band of hockey players disembarked at Bradbury Station near Clandeboye Avenue. Mr. Scourge himself made sure their duffle bags were taken from the baggage car and loaded onto a cart for delivery to the arena.

"Hell's bells," said Slim. "Isn't this the life? I don't even have to carry my equipment to the arena."

"Don't get used to it." Frank had consumed less wine than his friend.

The boys walked along Clandeboye Avenue. It was a bitter day and the road was covered with a thick sheet of ice polished by a north-west wind.

"I should have brought my speed skates," said Mike. "I could have raced to the arena in minutes."

"You're drunk," said Friddy.

"At least I can walk a straight line. The rest of you are staggering," retorted Mike.

When the boys reached the arena, they saw a crowd lined up on Fox Street waiting to purchase tickets for the big game. The Alexandra rink built in 1907 in the center of Selkirk was one of the most up-to-date arenas in western Canada. Constructed of arched wood beams, it enclosed an ice surface of 80 feet by 180 feet, not far off the so-called regulation size of the rinks in Montreal and Toronto. The Alexandra's owner boasted that teams from all parts of southern Manitoba came to play at his rink.

The boys were ushered into the arena by a representative of the Independent Hockey League.

"Well, isn't this hoity-toity," said Slim.

A young man carrying skates and a hockey stick heard Slim.

"What did you say?" he asked.

"I said this is an impressive arena," said Slim.

"Damn right it is," said the boy. "Best rink in western Canada."

Slim looked the fellow over. He was of average height with thick blond hair slicked back off his forehead. His prominent ears stuck out at right angles to his head, giving the impression he might take flight at any moment.

"And you'd be?" asked Slim.

"Crutchy Morrison, center for the Selkirk Fishermen. The rest of the lads will be here in a minute."

Sure enough, a group of tough looking young men entered the rink. The most remarkable member was skinny, had short black hair and a thick scar over his right eye.

"That's one of my mates, Bullet Joe Simpson. We plan to make fish soup out of you guys."

The Falcons looked over the opposition. The Selkirk Fishermen were indeed a rugged bunch of individuals. The only member of the team who offered his hand was a short fellow with red hair called Harry Oliver, who was of Icelandic descent.

"Welcome to Selkirk," he said.

Oliver showed the Falcons to their dressing room, a cold, inhospitable area with oak benches in the middle and wooden cupboards along the wall to store their clothes. There was a lot of banter among the boys as they changed into their hockey attire.

"Hey, Slim," said Goodman, "Your socks don't match. I thought you were getting a new pair."

"I can't afford a new pair, you dope. How would you like me to sock you in the eye so your eyes don't match?"

"Fine," said Goodman, taking up a boxing stance. "Give it your best shot."

The two boys sparred playfully with each other, dancing about the room knocking over duffle bags and clothing. Their teammates cheered as the two boxers pretended to land blows on each other.

"Keep your right up, Mike," yelled Bobby.

"Watch his left hook, Slim!" called Frank. In the midst of the melee, a referee poked his head through the doorway: "Five minutes to game time."

The teammates scrambled to find their skates, newspaper pads, and sticks that had scattered in the mock battle. They finished dressing hurriedly and trekked down a dark hall that led to the playing surface. They were astonished by the size and volume of the crowd. The arena was packed to capacity; only a small group of fans appeared to be cheering for the Falcons. Frank thought he noticed Steamer Maxwell and another man among them. He wondered if Steamer had been on the train with the diehard Winnipeg spectators who followed the Falcons on every road trip.

Frank made a couple of circuits around the rink and noticed how unsteady his legs felt. He cursed the big meal at lunch and the amount of wine he'd drunk with it.

The referee rang his bell and the players lined up at center for the face-off.

The puck was dropped. Frank's vision was blurry as he tried to locate the black disc which slipped off his stick and was scooped up by Crutchy Morrison. He passed the puck back to Bullet Joe Simpson on defense who began a dazzling rush up the ice. His pace was exceptional. Even Goodman, the Falcon's speedy left winger, couldn't keep up to Bullet Joe. He stick handled around Konnie and Bobby on defense and ripped a wrist shot into the right corner of the net before the normally alert Byron saw the puck.

The audience was on its feet. One fan holding a megaphone walked a tightrope strung between posts, urging the Fishermen on to greater efforts.

"Let's hear it for the Bullet," he bellowed to the fans.

"Bullet! Bullet!" reverberated around the rink.

Frank was angry and apprehensive because he felt so unsteady and was gasping for breath. He also had a vicious headache centered behind his right eye.

"You Goolies are fish soup," said Crutchy as he lined up for the face-off with Frank.

The comment irritated Frank. He fought hard to win the draw when the puck was dropped. But Crutchy got control and rushed straight forward, knocking Frank off his feet as he blazed by. Crutchy dazzled the home town fans with a brilliant one-man rush that split Konnie and Bobby on defense. The rest of the Falcons were so far behind that no one was in position to help Wally in goal. Crutchy performed a double feint that left Wally sitting on the ice with the puck in the back of the net.

The Fishermen fans were on their feet. The man on the tightrope did a couple of deft jumps in the air to show his enthusiasm.

"Crutchy deserves his own Duchy!" roared the fans.

As the cheering continued, the Falcons gathered around Wally for a conference.

"I don't know about you fellows," said the goalie, "but I feel like hell. I can't focus on the game and my reflexes are slow."

"It's all that wine we drank on the train," said Slim. "I feel as if I'm skating in slow motion. Damn you, Woodman, why did you let us get drunk? I feel like puking."

Huck was about to mention that he had warned them not to drink so much when Frank cut in: "Cool down, Slim. It's not Huck's fault. We made pigs of ourselves and now we're going to pay for it. I just hope we get out of this game without injuries."

The referee rang his bell and the players lined up at center. This time when the puck was dropped Frank took a swipe at the puck and was lucky enough to get it over to Slim on the right wing. The long-legged winger carried the puck into the Fishermen's scoring zone with a couple of strides. Just as Slim was preparing to take a shot on goal, a huge spurt of vomit projected from his mouth, covering a Fisherman with half-digested food and wine. Slim dropped to his knees and continued to wretch on the ice. The Selkirk defenseman stood in disbelief, trying to wipe off the vomit with his glove. A shout of horror and merriment was exhaled by the spectators. Some were shaking their fists at Slim, while others were laughing. The referee continued to ring his bell to signal a stoppage of play.

Frank and the rest of the Falcons skated around Slim to protect him from angry spectators who threatened to climb on the ice and give Slim a beating.

"Slim, can you get up?" asked Frank.

"Yeh. Help me to the changing room. I can't play any more today."

"That's okay, Friddy's a good spare. He can play your position. Now let's get you out of here before they send a lynch mob."

The Fishermen continued to notch markers. With five minutes to go, Bullet Joe broke loose and carried the puck into the Falcons' scoring zone. His shot on goal was hard and high and caught Wally on the bridge of his nose. He was stunned for a moment and then fell to the ice.

Frank and Konnie assisted Wally to the dressing-room where a doctor examined the goalie. Wally's nose had been split open by the edge of the puck. The gash required 10 stitches and Wally was out of the game.

"I wish Babe were with us," said Frank to Konnie.

Babe Elliott was the Falcon's back-up goalie. Although rarely called upon to play, he worked out with the team and traveled to some of their road games. On this occasion he was at home in Winnipeg with a bad cold.

"We'll have to put Bobby in net," said Frank. "He's got good reflexes."

With four minutes to go in the contest and an untested goaltender protecting the citadel, the Falcons girded themselves for a relentless attack by the Fishermen. Led by Crutchy and Bullet Joe, the Selkirk team made rush after rush up the ice, firing shot after shot at the Falcons' goalie. But Bobby stood his ground. He refused to be cowed by the furious barrage of pucks that were fired at him from all areas of the ice. Heartened by Bobby's resolve, the Falcons fought back hard and with 10 seconds left in the game Frank intercepted a pass at center, charged into the Fishermen's zone, and scored on a quick shot as he was being knocked to the ice by a defenseman.

There was some subdued applause from a small group in the crowd which unfurled a Falcons' banner for the first time that day. Otherwise, the arena was silent. The Selkirk fans had been expecting a shut out. Frank's goal had robbed them of this glory and they were not pleased.

"Lucky shot, Goolie," yelled one of the fans who had threatened to beat up Slim.

On their way out of the arena, Frank and his teammates were hailed by Steamer Maxwell who appeared out of the crowd with a short, balding man in tow.

"Fredrickson, that was the worst goddam hockey I've ever witnessed. What the hell was wrong with you boys? Did you all have the flu?"

"We learned a lesson today, Mr. Maxwell," said Frank.

"What did you learn?"

"Never drink during the hockey season."

Steamer looked angry but kept his thoughts to himself.

"I brought a friend with me who is an admirer of yours, Fredrickson. But after today's game he may have changed his mind."

Everyone turned to look at Steamer's friend.

"Boys," said Steamer, "I want you to meet Billy Finlay, the sports editor of the Manitoba Free Press."

The teammates were impressed. They knew Finlay by reputation but had never met him in person. Finlay shook hands and then lit a Philip Morris cigarette, sucking smoke into his lungs as he appraised the Falcons.

"Steamer tells me that wasn't the best hockey you lads are capable of. And it's a good thing. Aside from Fredrickson's goal, it was the worst bloody game I've ever witnessed. I'm looking for a Manitoba Independent League team to write about. I hope to hell you show me some better stuff next time."

Frank and his teammates nodded their heads.

"Good," said Finlay, pulling a silver flask from his pocket. "Drink is death to hockey players but life everlasting to writers."

He swallowed a large gulp from the flask.

"Cheers, gentlemen. I'll look forward to your next game."

CHAPTER THIRTEEN

Winnipeg, April 1917

*B*ill Finlay remained a loyal fan and continued to write about the Falcons through the disastrous seasons of 1912 and 1913, when the team lost consistently to the Selkirk Fishermen. Finally in 1914-15 the Falcons gelled as a squad, winning the Manitoba Independent League title. But the Fishermen rebounded the following year and fought their way to the Canadian Amateur Championship with an Allan Cup victory. The Selkirk players were permitted to represent Manitoba in the championship because they had enlisted in the 61st Battalion and would serve king and country overseas in the Great War that had engulfed Europe.

Senior hockey throughout Canada came to a standstill as more and more young men enlisted in the Canadian forces and were shipped across the Atlantic to fight the Hun armies advancing through Belgium and France.

The CPR station at Main and Higgins was packed with men in military uniforms surrounded by relatives, sweethearts and other well-wishers. The 223rd Overseas Battalion, composed partly of second-generation Icelandic men from Manitoba, was one of the last to board the train to Halifax. From there, the soldiers would sail to England to join the war against the Germans.

Frank and his sister Sarah hugged. The conductor called "all aboard."

"Oh, Frank, I love you so much. Do be careful over there," said Sarah.

"Don't worry, Sis. I've got your Gimli stone. As long as I have it, we'll both be safe."

They embraced one last time. Frank kissed his mother and shook hands with his father and younger brother. To Frank's surprise and joy, Bea Peterson suddenly arrived to see him off.

"Goodbye, Frank. Take care," she said, holding out her hand.

Frank ignored her hand and fully embraced her.

"Thank you so much for coming, Bea."

Slim, Huck, Friddy and Mike stood to one side. They were too young to enlist and resented they would not be joining the rest of the team on this grand adventure.

"C'mon, Frank," yelled Konnie from the door of the train. "You'll be considered AWOL if you miss your ride to Halifax."

As the train began to move, Frank jumped aboard. His sister ran after him.

"Frank, your violin!"

Frank reached down and grabbed the handle of the violin case.

"Thanks, Sis, I love you," called Frank.

From open windows, Konnie, Bobby, Wally, and Frank waved to their friends. It was a warm day in April. The breeze felt good on Frank's face as he lingered at the window watching his dear sister, parents, and friends. Then the locomotive turned a bend and his family was lost from sight. The train moved across the flat prairie east of Winnipeg and began to encounter the first granite boulders marking the edge of the Canadian Shield. Frank wondered how his life would change when he reached England. He and Konnie had decided to join the Royal Flying Corps. The commanding officer of the 223rd Battalion promised the boys they would be allowed to enlist at the RFC Headquarters in London. From London, they would be shipped to Egypt for flight training. Bobby and Wally had elected to remain with the 223rd, an infantry battalion scheduled to see active duty in France and Belgium.

"I guess that's the end of the Falcons," said Slim sadly. He turned to leave the station, unhappy to be left behind.

"Don't be so gloomy," retorted Mike. "Our friends will come back."

"I pray they'll return," said Slim. "But will the Falcons?"

CHAPTER FOURTEEN

Winnipeg, Spring 1919

*O*n the platform of the CPR station stood a crowd of young men, all of whom looked familiar to Frank and yet, all looked a little different.

He jumped from the moving train and was embraced by Slim who was six inches taller. The lanky right-winger shook his friend's hand.

"Look at you, Slim. You've grown a foot since I last saw you," said Frank. "With that curly black hair, you look like a matinee idol."

"You don't look so bad yourself, Frank. You've filled out in all the right places," said Slim, appraising his friend's broad shoulders, slim waist, and powerful legs.

Konnie walked up to Frank, lifting him off the ground in a powerful bear hug.

"It's about time the Royal Air Corps released you, Frank. I've been home from Egypt for a couple of weeks."

Konnie had always been a big lad, but now he was a man of strength and stature. Like Slim, he was over six feet tall, but he also possessed the physique of a professional wrestler.

Bobby jumped up on Konnie's shoulders so he could say hello to Frank.

"Hi ya, Frank. Did you meet any good looking birds in Scotland?"

"None that I'll tell you about, Jumping Jack," laughed Frank. "How was your time in the infantry?"

Bobby lowered himself from Konnie's shoulders and shrugged off the question.

Wally stepped out of the crowd and, in his quiet way, extended his hand to Frank.

"Good to see you alive and well," said Wally, who had seen extensive action in the battles of Amiens, Arras and Cambrai.

Mike, Friddy, and Huck pushed their way through the crowd.

"Frank!" cried the ebullient Mike. "It's great to have you back."

Friddy and Huck also offered congratulations.

"You wouldn't believe what Woodman did," said Mike. "He ran away from home to join the army. The recruiting sergeant took one look at him and called his parents."

Huck looked unabashed.

"You know me, Frank. I always want to be part of the action."

Frank smiled at the three younger players.

"I hear you guys have been chewing up the junior hockey league while we've been overseas," he said. "It sounds as if we've returned just in time to establish a dynasty."

"Dynasty!" cried Mike. "I like the ring of the word."

At that moment, Bea Peterson stepped forward.

"Hello, Frank," she said. "I've come to offer my condolences on the death of your dear sister, Sarah."

Frank bowed his head. In the joy of homecoming, he had not thought about his sister's premature death during the flu pandemic of 1918. He took Bea's hand and then embraced her.

"Bless you for your kind thoughts, Bea. My sister had a good friend in you. I wish she had had a more trustworthy friend in me," Frank said.

"What are you talking about?" asked Bea.

"Nothing," he said. Something had happened overseas that Frank would never reveal to Bea. He knew it was madness but, all the same, he blamed himself for his sister's death and he had tried to bury his grief along with his sister's memory.

—————•◦•—————

It was May, 1918 and Frank and Konnie stood on the dock at the Port of Alexandria waiting for Frank to board the troop ship *Leasowe Castle*. The ship was en route from Egypt to Marseille where Frank would board a train to Edinburgh. He had been assigned new duties as a flight instructor for the Royal Air Corps in Scotland.

"She looks a worthy tub. I'm sure she'll get you to Marseille," said Konnie. He noted that most of the soldiers climbing the gangways wore the insignia of the Warwickshire Yeomanry.

"As long as the bloody Huns don't torpedo her," laughed Frank.

"Take care of yourself, Frank," said Konnie, shaking his friend's hand.

Frank boarded the *Leasowe Castle* with hope in his heart. He had just received a short letter from his mother about the flu pandemic that had taken the lives of thousands of Winnipeggers but spared the Fredrickson family: "So far our family has been spared the curse by praying devoutly and attending church on Sunday. Your sister remains frail but, praise God, healthy. Mr. Bardal's Little White Hearse has visited hundreds of homes in the Icelandic neighborhood. It is everyone's greatest fear that one day the hearse will pull up at their house. God love you, Mother."

Frank reread the note as the ship weighed anchor and headed into the glittering expanse of the Mediterranean Sea. It was reassuring to know his family was safe and healthy in Winnipeg.

The second day at sea Frank stood on the deck of the *Leasowe Castle* and watched a school of bottle-nosed dolphins frolic in the sea, their torpedo-shaped bodies perfectly adapted to race through the azure water.

The peace of the moment was shattered by a siren.

"All hands to battle stations!"

A naval officer sprinted up a flight of metal stairs to the bridge.

"What's happening?" asked Frank.

"Torpedoes!"

The ship's deck shuddered as an explosion ripped through the port bow.

"We're hit! Man the lifeboats!" an officer bellowed through a megaphone.

Frank pushed through sailors and soldiers on the main deck. He fought his way to his cabin three decks below. There was already a foot of water around his feet when he forced open the door. His violin case floated in salt water. He opened it, checked inside to make sure his Gimli stone was in its usual place next to his violin. The instrument was there, but the stone was missing.

"It can't be lost. I promised Sarah no harm would come to her as long as I had the stone."

He searched the bunks, got down on his knees to examine the floor.

A warrant officer entered the cabin. "Sir, you must leave at once. Captain Holl has ordered all hands to abandon ship."

"I can't leave until I find something," said Frank.

"I have orders to shoot any person who will not vacate the ship in an orderly fashion."

The sailor pulled a revolver from a holster and pointed it at Frank.

"Are you insane?" asked Frank. "You can't shoot me."

"I can and I will," said the officer.

Frank cast one last desperate look around the cabin, then left with the sailor who ushered him into a lifeboat.

A lieutenant commander, the only senior officer to survive the sinking of the *Leasowe Castle*, had organized the lifeboats into a small flotilla so they would be easier to spot by search planes. Frank sat despondently in a boat with his violin in his lap.

"How about playing us a song?" asked a thin sailor with an Irish accent. "Danny Boy is one of my favorites."

Frank put the violin to his chin and ran the bow across the strings. It wasn't long before all the sailors in the flotilla began to sing the lyrics to the ancient Celtic melody. Tears fell from Frank's eyes as the lifeboats floated into darkness.

The flotilla was rescued two days later by a Japanese destroyer. It was on board the ship that Frank received a terse telegram from home: "Sarah passed away two days ago. May God help us all. Mother and Father."

Frank read the telegram, crushed it into a ball and threw it overboard.

"I've failed you, dear Sarah. I promised that no harm would come to you as long as I had the Gimli stone. Will you ever forgive me?"

———•+•———

Frank noticed that Bea had become a handsome young woman. She was tall and slender with the long, manicured hands of a pianist. The severe, pursed look around her lips had softened, replaced by a milder more sensitive mouth that was soft and beckoning.

"Look at you, Frank Fredrickson," she finally said, embarrassed by Frank's open appraisal. "You left a boy and you've returned a man. You don't seem nearly the show off you used to be."

Frank smiled at this indiscretion.

"I'm 24 years of age, Bea. I should be a man. War can bring out the worst and the best in a person."

She offered him her arm. "I dare say it's brought out the best in you, Frank."

CHAPTER FIFTEEN

*T*he group, including Bea, walked along Main Street. Frank was astonished to see the charred remains of an overturned streetcar in the middle of the street, close to City Hall.

"It seems the war is being fought on this continent, too," he remarked. "What's been happening during my absence?"

"It's the Bolshies," said Mike. "They're trying to start a revolution right here in Winnipeg and Slim is aiding and abetting them."

Everyone turned to look at the handsome right-winger.

"That's a load of manure," he said. "All I've done is hand out a few of J. S. Woodsworth's pamphlets to make some money. And besides I think he's on our side, even if he is a Bolshie."

"You see," cried Mike. "Slim's a card-carrying Red."

Slim lost his patience and took a swing at Goodman. The round house right passed harmlessly over Goodman's head because Slim was a foot taller than his opponent. Mike was about to retaliate with an uppercut of his own when Frank spoke up.

"Both of you stow it! We're friends not enemies. We all belong to the same team. We've got to start acting in a disciplined manner if we're ever going to achieve anything worthwhile."

The group fell silent.

"And just what team would you be talking about?" asked Goodman.

"The Falcons, of course," said Frank.

There was another silence as the boys considered Frank's words.

"You must be kidding," said Bobby. "Four of us haven't been on skates since we went overseas three years ago."

Frank looked at each member of the team before he spoke.

"I had lots of time to think on the train from Halifax to Winnipeg and my plan is to rebuild the Winnipeg Falcons."

The boys looked at Frank in disbelief as he unhooked a chain from around his neck and held up a gold amulet with a Viking warrior embossed on the surface.

"This will be our source of strength and inspiration. It's a replacement for something I can never fully replace. Anyone who wants to be a part of the new Falcons should step forward now and touch the amulet."

Wally was the first to grasp the amulet, followed soon by the rest of the teammates. They stood in a circle and locked hands together while Goodman cried out: "When falcons fly, the heroes of Valhalla cheer."

"This calls for a celebration!" shouted Bobby.

Frank turned to Bea, kissed her on the cheek before following his teammates into the McLaren Hotel.

"Thank you for being Sarah's dear friend and for meeting me at the station," he said.

Bea blushed and looked down at the sidewalk.

"It was no trouble, Frank. I must get home now."

Frank called after her.

"Will you have dinner with me some evening?"

"Yes. I'd like that," she said.

CHAPTER SIXTEEN

*T*he hotel's beverage room overflowed with men smoking cigars, chewing tobacco, and quaffing pints of draft beer. A polished mahogany bar, the longest in western Canada if the McLaren brothers were to be believed, ran the length of the dingy establishment. Sawdust covered the floor to absorb spit, spilt beer and mud tracked in from the street. The boys had to push their way through the crowd to get to the bar.

"What'll it be gentlemen?" asked Archie McLaren.

"Draft all around," said Frank.

While McLaren drew the beer from a keg, the boys found a table that was just being vacated by a crowd of men in business suits. One of them nodded at Frank and extended his hand.

"Welcome home, Fredrickson. You probably won't remember me. I'm Billy Finlay of the Free Press."

"Mr. Finlay. Of course I remember you. You traveled to Selkirk to watch one of our games against the Fishermen and you wrote stories about us even though we didn't give you much to write about."

Finlay reached into his vest pocket, pulled out a silver flask and took a gulp. He offered it to Frank who took a polite sip.

"Damn right I wrote about you boys. Too bad you had to go to war and break up the team. The Falcons had the makings of a fine hockey squad. I've kept my eye on Goodman, Halderson, Fridfinnson and Woodman since you older boys went overseas. They've been playing some excellent junior hockey with the Young Men's Lutheran Club."

Frank was pleased.

"How good are they?" he asked.

Finlay scratched the top of his head.

"I'd say they're as good as any of the players in the City League. It's a shame the Falcons never really got a chance to show their stuff," said Finlay. "I'd be willing to back a team like that."

Frank felt his pulse quicken.

"This is a remarkable coincidence," he said. "We came here to discuss re-forming the Falcons."

"You don't say," said Finlay, who reached into his jacket pocket for a notebook and pencil. "This is news. Tell me all about it, Fredrickson."

Falcons To Fly Again
To petition City League for a berth in Senior Division

By Billy Finlay

The Falcon Hockey Club which has been dormant since the winter of 1915-16 owing to practically all the members going overseas will reorganize this year with a bang. Officials and members of the Icelandic club are very enthusiastic over the game, and the club hopes to enjoy a wonderful revival. With all of its old players home once more and being strengthened by several youngsters who developed into junior stars during the war years, the Falcons are in position to place a fast team on the ice next winter. It is the intention of the club to petition the Winnipeg Hockey League for a berth in the city's senior division. Frank Fredrickson, captain and center, says their reorganization work will be completed by the end of June.

It can be confidently stated that none of the proposed senior clubs possesses as much inherent strength as the Falcons or are more fitted to worthily uphold the honor of hockey in Manitoba.

———•◦•———

M ac MacPherson, the richest man in Winnipeg and the director of the City Hockey League, was in a foul mood.

"I'm going to crush these Icelandic ne'er-do-wells once and for all!" yelled the fat man, as he strode across the Persian carpet in his office facing Main Street. "How dare those Goolies make application to join the city's senior hockey rank?"

Seated in leather chairs surrounding MacPherson's massive rosewood desk were his secretary, Art Snively, and officials of the City Hockey League. They sat quietly while the big man lumbered about the room, knocking over Louis XlV chairs and smashing his fist into the paneled walls.

"Excuse me, Mac," said Snively, staring at MacPherson through his thick oval glasses. "I think I know how to prevent the Goolies from entering our league or any league for that matter."

MacPherson looked at the small man with contempt.

"It's Mr. MacPherson to you, Snively. I don't pay you to think. I pay you to take orders!" MacPherson swatted at Snively's shiny head with his fleshy hand.

Snively ducked.

"But Mr. MacPherson, it's a good plan, worthy of you, sir."

MacPherson was suddenly interested.

"Worthy of me, you say. Well, okay then, let's hear it, but it'd better be good."

Snively stared at some notes he had been scribbling on a pad of vellum paper.

"I suggest we invite the Falcons' former allies in the Independent

League to join the City League. Brandon and Selkirk have been badgering us for years to get berths."

A smile formed on MacPherson's jowly face. He stuck a finger in his mouth to dislodge a scrap of meat stuck between his molars.

"Go on, Mr. Snively." He extricated the offal and flicked it against the wall.

"Well, if Brandon and Selkirk join us to form a new five-team City League, the Falcons would be left out in the cold, if you catch my humor, sir, with no one to play against."

"Left out in the cold, indeed!" MacPherson broke into a booming laugh.

"I like this plan, Snively. I'll call it my own when I tell the lads at the Manitoba Club about it. Now all of you get the hell out of my office. I have a phone call to make."

MacPherson flipped through an address book. He was looking for Billy Holmes' phone number. Holmes owned the Amphitheatre arena in which the City League practiced and played most of its games. MacPherson rang the number and drummed his manicured nails against his desk while he waited for an answer.

"Holmes speaking."

"Billy. It's MacPherson. I've got some wonderful news. You're going to make piles of dough this year and I'm going to skim a little extra off the top."

There was silence at the other end of the line.

"What are you scheming now?"

MacPherson admired his immaculate hands before answering.

"There will be five teams in the City League this season. Selkirk and Brandon will be persuaded to join our little combine of the Monarchs, Winnipegs, and Victorias. The Falcons will not be invited to join us."

There was another silence while Holmes considered the proposal.

"Are you crazy, MacPherson? Selkirk and Brandon will never abandon the Falcons. I don't think you understand men like Dave Morrison and Harry Stuart. They're honorable men first and managers second. They'll remain loyal to the Falcons no matter what you offer them."

"Loyalty is such a pitiful word, Billy. When it comes to money, power and prestige, every man is willing to sell his soul. Believe me, I know."

Holmes laughed scornfully. He was one of the few businessmen in Winnipeg who at times attempted to stand up to MacPherson.

"I guess you would know, Mac."

MacPherson sneered.

"Contempt doesn't become you, Billy boy. And don't forget who's holding the mortgage on your precious Amphitheatre," said MacPherson.

Holmes leaned back on a chair in his office thinking about MacPherson's blackmail. The fat bastard would make good on his threat to foreclose on the Amphitheatre's mortgage. And the ruthless fraud had enough money and influence to ensure that no one else in Winnipeg, banks included, would dare to pick up the mortgage. Billy Holmes felt queasy. He had spent years building the Amphitheatre into one of Winnipeg's most prestigious rinks. And he had six children and a wife to support.

CHAPTER EIGHTEEN

*B*illy Finlay had a difficult time persuading Steamer Maxwell to become the full-time coach of the reorganized Falcons. Maxwell was a logical choice because he had occasionally worked with the team before the war. But Steamer was fed up with hockey and more inclined to pursue a career in baseball because the game was his second love. His spectacular career as a rover with the Winnipeg Monarchs had ended in 1915 with an Allan Cup victory. A few weeks later, Maxwell hung up his skates in disgust when he discovered some amateur teams were paying their players.

"I bought my own skates and equipment when I played," Steamer ranted to Finlay, as they sat in the Free Press building one sultry day in August 1919. "I won't coach a team that receives money to play hockey. It's ruining the game."

Finlay sat back in his oak armchair, lit another cigarette, and watched the smoke hang in the dank air as he exhaled.

"You don't have to worry about the Falcons and cash," he laughed. "That organization is so poor the players all wear different uniforms."

"Perhaps," said Steamer. "But the National Hockey League is shelling out big money to professional players. It won't be long before amateur hockey throughout the country is tainted by the allure of dollar signs."

Billy Finlay was more optimistic about the outlook for amateur sport. He believed the line between an amateur and a professional athlete could be maintained as long as corporations were prevented from sponsoring individuals or teams holding amateur status. But he couldn't win Maxwell over to his side.

"What will it take for me to convince you the Falcons' administration will not pay their players?" asked Finlay.

"A written guarantee from you and Hebbie Axford," declared Maxwell.

"What about uniforms?" asked Finlay. "These boys own their skates and sticks, nothing else."

"Okay. I concede they'll need uniforms to compete at the senior level. But that's it." Maxwell folded his arms over his chest.

"Have we got a deal?" asked Finlay.

"Let's call it a temporary understanding," said Maxwell. He stood up to leave.

On his way out of the Free Press building, Steamer thought about the challenge ahead. Fredrickson, Johannesson, Byron and Benson had not been on skates since they went overseas three years ago. They were out of shape and their skills needed re-honing. On the other hand, the younger players were in shape but lacked the discipline their older teammates had learned in the armed forces. Hockey, he knew, was a game of strength, skill, and above all, discipline.

CHAPTER NINETEEN

The early morning workouts became a familiar sight to residents of Goolie Crescent. At 6 a.m. sharp, Steamer Maxwell met the Falcons at the corner of Sargent and Victor and led them on an eight mile run that wended through the heart of Little Iceland. Residents stopped their chores to watch the team jog by. The overcrowded neighborhood had continued to expand as new settlers arrived from Iceland daily. As well, Icelanders who had immigrated to Manitoba in 1875 and settled along a narrow tract of land about 40 miles north of Winnipeg, called New Iceland, had been lured to the city by promises of better jobs and prosperity. In the early decades of the 20th century, Winnipeg was a boom town. It was the hub of the grain and wholesale industries and a natural transportation center because of its location in the middle of the country.

"Okay, boys, that's enough moping, let's pick up the pace!" Steamer blew his whistle.

"Frankie, this is killing me," said Slim.

"Why are you complaining Slim? I'm the one who is supposed to be out of shape."

"Hey, Slim," yelled Friddy from a few yards ahead. "There's that girl Olive you rescued at the Auditorium Arena."

The lanky right-winger tripped and fell at the mention of Olive. He had searched Little Iceland for the beautiful young woman ever since the encounter with Mr. Legge.

Slim picked himself up and looked to where Friddy had pointed. Sure enough, standing among a small crowd of spectators was Olive. Slim left his teammates and approached the young woman.

"Olive," he said shyly. "I've never stopped looking for you. You never told me your last name."

"You never told me your name at all," said Olive, smiling up at the awkward young giant.

Steamer looked over his shoulder and saw Slim making small talk with a young woman. The irascible coach blew his whistle and marched over to where Slim and Olive stood spellbound.

"What in hell's name are you doing, Mr. Matinee Idol? Get back in line and keep your skinny ass moving!" Steamer smacked Slim on the seat with the flat of his hand.

"But coach," protested Slim. "I've been searching for this girl everywhere. I don't even know her last name."

"You can ask her when hockey season is over," said Steamer. He took Slim by the arm and dragged him back to the group of joggers.

"My last name is McKay," Olive called out.

"My name is Slim, Slim Halderson."

The smitten right-winger jabbered something to Steamer about how he intended to marry Olive.

"I don't give a damn who you marry," said Steamer. "That was a breach of discipline and it will be your last if you plan to remain a member of this team. Do I make myself clear, Mr. Halderson?"

The teammates resumed their positions and Maxwell increased the pace to a full sprint.

CHAPTER TWENTY

While Frank and his teammates prepared for the upcoming season, a fight brewed between the City League and representatives of Brandon, Selkirk and the Falcons. The bad blood between the organizations finally became public in November when a series of articles appeared in the Free Press.

On November 3, a story by Billy Finlay announced that the Winnipeg League had refused to admit the three independent clubs into its ranks. As a result, a new Manitoba Hockey League, composed of the Falcons, Brandon, and Selkirk, was being organized for the 1919 season. On November 4, Finlay wrote:

Another Bomb Dropped on Senior Hockey Situation
Impossible to handle two leagues at the Amphitheatre, says Billy Holmes
—Winnipeg Senior City League to make overtures to Brandon and Selkirk

By Billy Finlay

Billy Holmes called representatives of the Winnipeg and Manitoba leagues together yesterday afternoon and told them plainly that it was impossible for him to handle the situation at the Amphitheatre under a two-league scheme. He issued the ultimatum that a single league was the only one he could handle at the Amphitheatre and that a five-team league was the only possible solution. It is not known whether Brandon and Selkirk will stick by their agreement with the Falcons, and as the Falcons were not mentioned in connection with the five-team league, it is just possible that the other two members of the Manitoba Hockey League will insist on the Falcons being a member of any league in which they play...

Hebbie Axford skimmed the article as he strode down Bannatyne Avenue on his way to a meeting with other representatives of the newly formed Falcon hockey club. Axford had recently returned from England as a member of the Royal Air Corps. He was a second-generation Icelandic immigrant who had been a staunch supporter of amateur hockey in Manitoba for many years and was now the president of the Falcons. While he read the Free Press story, Axford shook his head in disbelief.

He entered a compact red brick office building and climbed the stairs to the second floor where he knocked briefly and walked into the office of Colonel Marino Hannesson.

"Have you read the latest?" he asked, slamming the newspaper on a coffee table in the middle of the small room.

"I've read it," said Hannesson, seated at a small desk squeezed into a corner of the office.

Hannessson was the vice-president of the Falcons. He was a powerfully built man in his mid-40s with a jutting chin and broad nose that gave him a look of authority.

"I'm afraid our friend MacPherson has put pressure on Billy Holmes," said Hannesson.

"It must have been a lot of pressure," said a man seated quietly in a corner of the room.

"Holmes is not usually the type to acquiesce to MacPherson's demands," said Fred Thordarson, who was the Falcon's secretary-treasurer and had played on provincial championship Icelandic teams in the past.

Thordarson stood up. His hazel eyes sparked with intelligence.

"What kind of stick do you think MacPherson used to beat Holmes into submission?" asked Axford.

"Money," said Thordarson.

"You mean he bribed him?"

"No. Holmes would never take a bribe."

"What then?"

"I've been doing some research," said Thordarson. "You'll never guess who holds the mortgage on the Amphitheatre."

"I'll wager it's Mac MacPherson," said Colonel Hannesson.

"Exactly right," said Thordarson.

The colonel reached for the telephone.

"I think we should arrange a meeting with Mr. Holmes. We are not without friends and resources of our own."

CHAPTER TWENTY-ONE

*B*illy Holmes was overseeing the installation of new tiers of seats high up at the south end of the Amphitheatre when Colonel Hannesson, Fred Thordarson, and Hebbie Axford arrived for a meeting.

"I'll be right down," he called to the three men. They watched as he negotiated a long stretch of scaffolding that led to a flight of stairs. Holmes descended the stairs rapidly. He had strong legs and a barrel chest. In his youth, he had been known as "Scrapper" Holmes because of his prowess in the boxing ring. Now 40 years of age, he still kept himself in shape. His nose had been broken so many times that it arced permanently to the left side of his lined face.

Holmes led the men down a dark corridor that smelled of sweat. He directed them into his office, an unpretentious box of pine flooring and concrete walls; pictures of local hockey heroes festooned the walls including Dick Irvin, Joe Simpson, and Steamer Maxwell.

"Sit down, gentlemen." Holmes motioned to an assortment of stools and chairs that composed the office furniture.

Holmes looked at his guests through fatigued eyes. Though his physical strength was unwavering, he appeared tired and conflicted.

Colonel Hannesson was the first to speak.

"Mr. Holmes I'm not going to waste your time with unnecessary formalities, so I'll get to the point. "We've come here to ask you to allow two hockey leagues to operate in Winnipeg. As I'm sure you are aware, it's the only chance the Falcons will have to play at the senior level."

Holmes rubbed a scar that ran the length of his jaw.

"Believe me, gentlemen, I'd like to accommodate you, but there aren't enough days in a week for two leagues to practice and play games at the Amphitheatre."

Fred Thordarson spoke up.

"So you've told the media. But I beg to differ. There's no reason why the Winnipeg League could not play home games at the Amphitheatre on Thursday nights and practice here week-day evenings. In exchange, the Manitoba League would practice at another rink such as the Winnipeg and play their games at the Amphitheatre on Monday nights."

Holmes looked uncomfortable.

"That's quite impossible," he said. "Monday is reserved for public skating."

"Monday *evening* is reserved," retorted Thordarson, "but hockey games don't start until Monday night. Public skating is over by then."

Holmes continued to stroke the scar on his chin and stare at a wall behind Thordarson.

"The ice couldn't be cleaned in time for the start of the games. Public skaters leave the surface in an awful mess," he answered.

Thordarson looked desperately to his companions for support. Hebbie Axford got to his feet, walked up to Holmes' desk, and leaned over, looking the man in the eyes.

"Let's be frank, Billy. We know you're a good man and we also know you're in a jam. We're in a position to help you out."

Holmes scoffed.

"Help me," he laughed bitterly. "Gentlemen, you can't help me. I made my pact long ago."

Axford continued to stare at Holmes. It seemed that the man was on the point of tears.

"You don't know what he's like, what he's capable of," said Holmes.

"Billy," said Axford gently, "we know about MacPherson. We know he holds the mortgage on this building. Has he threatened to foreclose if you don't accommodate him?"

Holmes looked up. His bleary eyes began to clear and a little hope lit his face.

"How did you know?"

"We put two and two together," said Axford. "We knew he couldn't bribe you. It seemed logical that threatening to shut down your business was the only lever he had at his disposal."

Billy got up from his chair, looked gratefully at Axford and his companions.

"He said he'd close my Amphitheatre—I've got a wife and children to support— and make sure I'd never start another business in Winnipeg. I had no choice but to play his game!"

There was a knock on the door. It was opened slightly and a face peeked into the room.

"Excuse me gentlemen. I apologize for being late for our meeting. May I come in?"

Holmes looked relieved, as if he'd expected the devil himself to slip through the door.

"Come in," he said, regaining his composure. He stared at the stranger quizzically.

Colonel Hannesson made the introduction.

"Welcome, Halson," he said extending his hand to the stranger. "Halson, I want you to meet Billy Holmes, owner and operator of this magnificent arena."

"Mr. Holmes. It's a pleasure. My name is Halson Solmundson of Laycock, Solmundson & Levine. I'm a bit of a hockey aficionado myself," he said, shaking Holmes' hand while admiring the hockey photos on the walls.

"On the way in I noticed you're doing some renovations. Must be expensive," said Solmundson.

"Sure is," agreed Holmes. "I'm expanding from 3,000 to 6,000 seats. Senior hockey is a big draw in this town, as you know."

"Actually, that's why I've come to see you," he said. "My partners and I are strong believers in the game of hockey. In fact, we have a rather good team in the Lawyers' League this season."

"Didn't your team win the Lawyers' League championship a few years ago?" Holmes asked Solmundson.

"Damn right!" said the lawyer proudly. "It was in this building and it was a young Icelandic player who set us on the road to victory."

"I remember, now," said Holmes. "It was Frank Fredrickson. He played center."

"That's right," said Solmundson. "I still believe in that young man and so do my partners. That's why I'm here."

"I don't understand," said Holmes.

Solmundson gave him a reassuring smile and a roll of his eyebrow.

"Let's just say that my partners and I are in the market for a hockey arena. We want to purchase only the best. The Amphitheatre seems most promising. Of course, there would be a condition."

Holmes was stunned. He looked suspiciously at Solmundson.

"What's the condition?"

"The condition is that you allow two leagues to operate out of this rink, the City League and the Manitoba League. It would give the Falcons an opportunity to play hockey at the senior level."

Holmes thought about the proposal.

"If it were possible, I'd gladly let two leagues play at the Amphitheatre. But the decision isn't mine to make. Mac MacPherson will never sell this building and he'll crush me and the Amphitheatre before he lets the Falcons play senior hockey."

Solmundson smiled.

"Don't be so gloomy, Holmes. We've got MacPherson backed into his own end. If he tries to foreclose on your mortgage, we'll buy it and offer you a lower rate of interest, too. MacPherson may be a bastard, but he's not stupid. We've got him on the boards and he'll soon realize it. All you've got to do is publicly state that you've decided to let both leagues play at your rink. Buck up, man. Show MacPherson your spine."

Billy Holmes looked as if a punishing weight had been removed from his shoulders. A light that had been quenched suddenly rekindled in his fighter's eyes.

Herbert Hebbie Axford

Axford continued as president of the Falcons for many years after the team's Olympic victory. He had an exceptional war record. His heroic dogfights over France and Belgium in the Royal Flying Corps in WW I earned him the award of a Distinguished Flying Cross and a promotion to captain.

b. Glenboro, Manitoba 1893 d. Winnipeg 1974

Robert John Bobby Benson

Benson left Winnipeg in the fall of 1920 to play professional hockey with the Saskatoon Crescents. In 1922, he joined the Calgary Tigers of the Western Canadian Hockey League and remained with the team for three seasons. He played for the Boston Bruins of the NHL in the 1924/25 season, was traded to the Edmonton Eskimos in 1925/26, and to the Saskatoon Shieks midway through the season. Other teams he played for included the Moose Jaw Warriors of the Prairie League, and the Minneapolis Millers of the American Hockey Association. He retired from professional hockey in 1929 to become a carpenter in Winnipeg.

b. Regina 1894 d. Winnipeg 1965

Walter Wally Byron

Wally Byron continued to tend goal for the Winnipeg Falcons until 1923. Considered one of the best goalies in amateur hockey in Canada, he honed his catching skills during the off season as a baseball player. He was intrepid between the pipes. During the 1920 Allan Cup series, he received a laceration to his face from the edge of a puck that required nine stitches. At the Antwerp Olympics, he broke a finger when he reached out to catch a shot from a U.S. player that would have resulted in a sure goal. He registered three shut outs in the Allan Cup and Olympic tournaments. He later worked for North Star Oil in Prince Albert and Anglo-Canadian Oil in Brandon.

b. Winnipeg 1894 d. Winnipeg 1971

Frank Fredrickson

Fredrickson turned professional in 1920-21, playing with the Victoria Aristocrats, later Cougars, of the Pacific Coast League. In 1925, he and former Falcons' teammate, Slim Halderson led the Cougars to an upset Stanley Cup victory over the Montreal Canadians. In 1926-27, Fredrickson signed with Detroit for $6,000, making him the highest paid player in the National Hockey League. He became the league's first player-coach-manager with Pittsburgh in 1929. A knee injury ended his professional career in 1932. He became coach of the Princeton University Tigers in 1933, where he was a friend of Albert Einstein.

He moved to the west coast where he coached the Sea Island Flyers of the Royal Canadian Air Force. He coached the University of British Columbia hockey team for five seasons and in 1949-50 took the team to unprecedented victory over both Canadian and US college teams. Fredrickson was inducted into the Hockey Hall of Fame in 1958 and the UBC Sports Hall of Fame and Museum in 1983. The Falcons were inducted into the Manitoba Sports Hall of Fame and Museum in 1980 and the Canadian Olympic Hall of Fame in 2006.

He sat as a councillor for the city of Vancouver and was renowned for bridge and playing the violin. He married Bea Peterson in 1923.

b. Winnipeg 1895 d. Vancouver 1979

Kristjan Chris Fridfinnson

Fridfinnson continued to play amateur hockey in Winnipeg until 1929 when he was hired to coach the University of Alberta varsity hockey team. He was dubbed the "Miracle Man" for turning the Alberta team, a perennial loser, into a winning squad that advanced to Edmonton's city final in 1930/31. Due to poor health, he returned to Winnipeg in 1931 to pursue a career as an accountant. In 1937, he entered a Winnipeg hospital and never left, passing away two years later at age 40. He was inducted into the Manitoba Sports Hall of Fame and Museum in 1980 as a member of the Winnipeg Falcons.

b. Baldur, Manitoba 1899 d. Winnipeg 1939

William Bill Fridfinnson

Bill Fridfinnson played a major role in amalgamating Winnipeg's early Icelandic teams—the Athletic Club and the Viking Club—into the Winnipeg Falcons in 1910. Fridfinnson was appointed secretary of the Falcons for the 1910-11 season and remained in that position for many years. He escorted the team to the Antwerp Olympics where one of his main responsibilities was to chaperone the excited young players.

b. Bru, Manitoba 1890 d. Winnipeg 1941

Magnus Mike Goodman

Goodman refused numerous offers to play professional hockey, continuing his amateur career with the Winnipeg Falcons until 1921. He was Manitoba's speed skating champion in 1918, 1919 and 1920 and Canadian champion in 1920. He was also the Western Canadian champion swimmer in the mile and was offered a chance to compete in that event at the 1920 Summer Olympics. He turned it down as he could not afford to pay his way to the Canadian finals in Montreal. In 1938, he moved to Florida to found a hockey team, the Coral Gables Seminoles. In his later years, he ran the delivery service for a Miami dry cleaning company. Goodman was honored at the 1988 Olympics in Calgary as the last surviving member of the world's first Olympic gold hockey team.

b. Winnipeg 1899 d. Florida 1992

Harold Slim Halderson

Halderson signed a contract to play professional hockey with the Saskatoon Crescents in 1920. He moved to the Victoria Aristocrats, later Cougars, in 1921 and won a Stanley Cup in 1925 with former Falcons' teammate Frank Fredrickson. In the 1926/27 season, he played for both the Detroit Cougars and the Toronto Maple Leafs. In his hockey career, Halderson was affiliated with the Quebec Beavers, Newark Bulldogs, Kansas City Pla-Mors, Duluth Hornets, Tulsa Oilers, and Wichita Skyhawks. He retired from hockey in 1937 and took a job with the former Manitoba Liquor Commission in Winnipeg. He died in 1965 and as a member of the Winnipeg Falcons was inducted into the Manitoba Sports Hall of Fame and Museum in 1980. He married Olive McKay.

b. Winnipeg 1899 d. Winnipeg 1965

Konrad Konnie Johannesson

In 1925, Johannesson joined the Winnipeg Maroons of the Central Hockey League. The following two seasons he played for the Moose Jaw Maroons and then the Regina Capitals of the Pro Hockey League. In 1928, he accepted a one-year offer to play professionally in Seattle. From 1929 to 1934, he was manager and chief flying instructor at the Winnipeg Flying Club. During WW II, he operated the Johannesson Flying Service in Winnipeg, teaching Icelandic-speaking students to fly for the Royal Canadian Air Force. Three of these students later founded Loftleidir, now a part of Icelandair.

b. Argyle 1896 d. Winnipeg 1968

Frederick George Steamer Maxwell

Maxwell continued to coach amateur hockey until 1928 when he accepted a professional contract from the Maroons of the American Hockey Association. In 1930, he turned down a lucrative offer of $1,500 to coach the Toronto Maple Leafs. Maxwell won a second amateur hockey world title in 1935 when he piloted the Winnipeg Monarchs to the championship in Davos, Switzerland. Steamer also loved baseball and was a strong promoter of the Goldeyes, a baseball team organized in Winnipeg after WWII. He was elected to the Hockey Hall of Fame in 1962.

b. Winnipeg 1890 d. Winnipeg 1975

Gudmundur Gordon Sigurjonsson

Gordon Sigurjonsson, trainer and assistant coach of the 1920 Falcons, was an exceptional athlete who demonstrated the sport of glima (wrestling) at the London Olympic Games in 1908 as a member of the Icelandic team. Soon after, he moved to Canada and in 1916 went overseas to fight in Belgium and France. At the Antwerp Games, the Swedish hockey team was so impressed by Sigurjonsson's ability as a trainer it hired him to develop its track and field team at the Summer Olympics in Antwerp.

b. Sudur-Thingeyjarsysla, Iceland 1883 d. Reykjavik, Iceland 1967

Frederick Fred Thordarson

Fred Thordarson was on the executive of the 1920 Olympic world champion Falcons. He played on earlier Falcons teams and continued to work in an executive capacity for the club until its demise in the late 1930s. Thordarson wrote "The Romance of the Falcons," originally published in Canadian Sports and Outdoor Life and later in the 1996 and 2002 issues of The Icelandic Canadian. His memorable saga of the Falcons preserved the history of the team for future fans. Thordarson worked for the Royal Bank in Winnipeg for 44 years.

b. Winnipeg 1890 d. Winnipeg 1966

Alan Charles Huck Woodman

Woodman took a job at Eaton's, an opportunity offered to all the Falcons in recognition of their Allan Cup and Olympic victories. In 1922, he became captain of the Kenora Thistles, a senior team in the Thunder Bay Amateur Hockey Association. Woodman worked as branch manager of the International Paint Company in Winnipeg for 25 years until he retired in 1960.

b. Winnipeg 1899   d. Winnipeg 1963

The Winnipeg Falcons in front of the Amphitheatre in 1920 after defeating the Winnipeg Winnipegs 15-1 in a two-game series to determine the contender in the Western Hockey Final. Front row (left to right) Coach Steamer Maxwell, Bobby Benson, Frank Fredrickson, Mike Goodman and Wally Byron.Top row (left to right) President Hebbie Axford, Alan Woodman, Slim Halderson, Konnie Johannesson and Chris Fridfinnson.

Onward to victory souvenir postcard designed by Charlie Thorson, an Icelandic Canadian artist credited with drawing one of Walt Disney's most memorable characters, Snow White. The falcon is the bird of Iceland.

Winnipeg Falcons view the sites of London on their way to the Olympic hockey championships in Belgium in 1920.

Team Canada executive director Wayne Gretzky celebrates his team's Olympic gold victory at the 2002 games in Salt Lake City. The Canadian team was invited to Iceland House by hosts (left to right) Eric, Marno and Jaye Olafson. Team Canada players signed posters of the mural of the 1920 world champion Winnipeg Falcons seen in the background.

CHAPTER TWENTY-TWO

*I*t was a bitter night in mid-November when representatives of the City League and the Manitoba League met in MacPherson's office to discuss the dispute between the two organizations. MacPherson demanded the meeting be held in his office as he felt its opulence would intimidate the representatives of Brandon and Selkirk.

MacPherson watched the men gather. They were like so many pawns on a chess board to be manipulated at his command.

"Mr. MacPherson," said Art Snively. "Shall I offer the gentlemen a beverage?"

"Offer the members of the City League anything they want," said MacPherson. "The hicks and the Goolies can go without for the time being."

MacPherson sat back, sipped his drink, and considered his position. He held a strong hand. He was sure that Brandon and Selkirk would abandon the Falcons in favor of an opportunity to play in the coveted City League. But even if they decided to honor their pact with the Falcons and remain in the Manitoba League, they would never play senior hockey in the Amphitheatre—Billy Holmes would see to that. The old combine of the Victorias, Winnipegs, and Monarchs would have the premier rink to themselves. It would mean less revenue, considered MacPherson, but he was already rich. Power over the Goolies was what motivated him now.

Colonel Hannesson, Fred Thordarson, and Hebbie Axford found seats in the room near other representatives of the Manitoba League. Harry Stuart, manager of the Brandon Wheat Cities, and Dave Morrison, president of the Selkirk Fishermen, shook hands with the Icelanders.

Billy Finlay sat next to the door in case he needed to rush to the Free Press to report breaking news.

MacPherson opened the meeting by banging his right fist on his rosewood desk.

"Gentlemen," he began, rising dramatically to make a show of buttoning his black silk suit. "We are here today to discuss a most important issue, an issue that I'm sure will be resolved to the benefit of the important people in this room." He nodded in the direction of the contingent representing the City League. In their midst sat Billy Holmes, his face serene and inscrutable.

MacPherson continued. "I now call upon Mr. Dave Morrison to inform us of his decision concerning our invitation to the Selkirk Fishermen to join a five-team City League."

Morrison made his way to the front of the room. He did not seem the least bit intimidated by MacPherson or his fancy office. He was a straightforward man who came from a family of hard-working farmers, fishermen, and hockey players. Indeed, his siblings Bobby and Crutchy Morrison played goal and forward respectively for the Selkirk senior team.

Morrison faced the men in the room, a grin discernible on his handsome face; his dark eyes fixed on MacPherson.

"Gentlemen," he said, "as far as I personally am concerned, I will not throw down the Falcons, even if our boys never play another game. We were forced into this by the Winnipeg League and we will play marbles before giving in to the Winnipeg League."

Morrison returned to his seat. There was loud applause from the Icelanders. MacPherson looked as if he'd been skewered in the gut with the blade of a hockey stick. His hands shook so badly he spilled the remains of his drink as he stood to announce the next speaker, Harry Stuart of Brandon.

Stuart was a grain farmer with big calloused hands and a bronze complexion burned into his skin by years of toil in the sun. He surveyed the men in the room before he spoke.

"I'm just a farm boy," he began, "so you gentlemen will have to excuse my way of speaking. My father, a fine man, taught me to speak my mind plain and simple so that's what I aim to do. He also taught me to be loyal to my friends. As far as the Brandon club is concerned, the members of the City League can take their offer and shove it where the sun refuses to shine. We will not abandon the Falcons."

MacPherson leapt out of his soft chair like a man poked in the rear with a pitch fork.

"So that's how you want it!" he screamed. "Well, I don't give a damn about you hicks and your second-rate teams. The Winnipeg League will be stronger without you."

He sat down, shaking. Snively poured him a double scotch which MacPherson downed in a gulp. MacPherson relaxed. The game, he thought, was not lost. Billy Holmes would wipe the smug smiles off their faces when he announced his intention to allow only the City League to operate in the Amphitheatre.

All the men scrutinized Holmes as he picked his way through the crowded room. The manager of the Amphitheatre was well-known to everyone present. The men remarked to each other how well Holmes looked, as if he had discovered the secret of youth, suddenly looking 30 years of age instead of 40. But it was more than that. There was a serenity and assurance about the manager that the men had never noticed before.

Holmes cleared his throat and began to speak.

"I've worked a good part of my life to make the Amphitheatre one of the premier hockey venues in Winnipeg. Next to my family, the rink is most precious to me. I have recently expanded my arena to include 3,000 more seats to accommodate the growing number of people in this province who love hockey and who want to watch the game in a first-rate rink. These fans deserve to see the best teams face off in the finest facility available..."

"Get on with it Holmes!" yelled MacPherson, impatient to watch the faces of his opponents when the bomb was dropped.

"For this reason," continued the manager, "I have decided to allow two leagues to operate in the Amphitheatre this season."

The room exploded in noise and confusion. Billy Finlay made a quick exit to file his report, while representatives of the City League voiced their opposition by calling Holmes a "disgrace to the city and to the gentleman's sport of hockey."

MacPherson stood up, his fists raised, his cheeks flushed with rage, his body trembling. He moved toward Holmes like a defenseman about to level a pesky little forward. When MacPherson reached out to grab the insubordinate manager by the neck, the former boxer pivoted on his toes, unleashing a wicked right to the jaw that dropped the fat man like a goalie taking a puck to the chin.

The Icelanders hustled the feisty manager out of the room.

"Did I cold cock the bastard?"

"Indeed you did," said Colonel Hannesson as the triumphant group left the building.

Local Hockey Squabble Settled Yesterday With Two Leagues in Operation

By Billy Finlay

The hockey war is no more. Peace was declared last night between the rival factions and everything is serene in local hockey circles once again. Manager Billy Holmes, of the Amphitheatre rink, acted as peace-maker when he agreed to handle both the Winnipeg and Manitoba leagues at his rink this winter. The Manitoba League season opener on December 15 will see the Falcons pitted against their old rivals the Selkirk Fishermen. The Canadian Amateur Hockey Association surprised local puck chasers by announcing that the winner of the Manitoba League championship will play off with the champions of the City League to decide which team will represent the province in the Western Hockey Final in early March.

CHAPTER TWENTY-THREE

*T*he Falcons lost the opening game of the 1919-20 season to the indomitable Selkirk Fishermen. Frank and the rest of his teammates saw their dream of a miraculous comeback year dashed before it began.

Steamer Maxwell's eyes were popping out of his head and the veins stood out on his temples. He trekked back and forth in the dressing room stopping before Slim.

"You, Matinee Idol! Do you know why we lost tonight's game?"

Slim stared at Maxwell's feet.

"We didn't play as a team," the right-winger mumbled.

"Speak up, Halderson. I can't hear you."

"We didn't play as a team," yelled Slim.

"Wrong! You didn't play like a member of a team."

Slim scratched his nose as he tried to avoid Maxwell's eyes.

"How many times," continued Steamer, "have I told you to stick to your position on right wing?"

"Many times, sir."

"Many! I'd say about a thousand times. And still on every rush you persisted in skating into the left-winger's corner. How many times have I told you to stay in your lane—to play your position!"

"About a thousand times, sir."

"Don't mock me, Halderson. If you want to remain a member of this squad you will respect me, listen to me, and above all do exactly as I say. Is that clear?"

"Yes, sir," said Slim quietly.

Maxwell moved along the line of players stopping in front of Goodman.

"Goodman," he said, pointing an index finger at the left-winger. "Were you a little under the weather tonight? Poor boy has a little head cold, perhaps? Something was wrong, because I've seen girls skate faster than you did tonight. Do you know why I find that so deplorable, Goodman?"

"Not exactly, sir," said Mike.

"I find it deplorable," said Maxwell, "because you just won the Canadian speed skating championship. You are the fastest man on the ice and this team depends on you to back check for a full 60 minutes. If you're not up to that, you can pick up your skates and catch a train to Lake Placid."

Goodman glared at Maxwell.

"I skated hard tonight, sir."

"No you didn't," retorted the coach. "You skated like you had a shot-put sewn into the seat of your pants. I suggest you remove it before the next game or it will be your last with the Falcons."

Maxwell continued to stalk his players.

"Fredrickson," he said stopping before the captain and center of the team. "You're a smart guy. Why hasn't it occurred to you that a shot on goal is preferable to a bullet drive that misses the net completely? You're the most gifted player on this team and yet you're so self-involved that you attempt to impress the audience with your wild wrist shot. The pretty little women in the crowd may be impressed, Fredrickson, but I'm not! Next game you might consider passing the puck to a teammate before you shoot it wide of the net."

Steamer's anger did not abate as he confronted his defensemen.

"After tonight, I'm going to christen you the Bumble Brothers! I've never witnessed such sloppy defense work. How many times did Joe Simpson or Harry Oliver split you apart like you were a couple of wooden dummies? And how many times did you give the puck away in your own end? I've seen junior defensemen play better hockey."

Konnie and Bobby hung their heads as Maxwell continued his tongue lashing.

"Are you listening to me?" he said, grabbing Bobby by the chin.

"Yes, coach," mumbled the diminutive defenseman.

Maxwell kicked Konnie in the shin to ensure the big man was also paying attention.

"I expect you two guys to stop the opposition every time they skate into the scoring zone. I don't care how you do it. If Benson has to jump on a player's back to haul him down, then so be it. And don't poke check! Johannesson, you're a big man. Use your body to take out an opponent."

There was silence in the dressing room as he continued his rounds. He came to a halt in front of Friddy and Huck, regarding them pensively before he spoke.

"You two boys played well tonight. You didn't get a lot of ice time, but when you were out there you did everything well. You played your positions, passed the puck, and showed the kind of team spirit that I want the Falcons to be known for. Good work gentlemen. Keep it up and you'll be playing regular shifts."

The last man to be scrutinized was Wally. The soft-spoken goalie kept his head up as Maxwell approached the bench where he was seated.

"Stand up, Mr. Byron."

Wally got to his feet. His teammates watched anxiously.

"Gentlemen," said Maxwell, "this young man is the reason the Fishermen scored only five goals this evening instead of 25. Mr. Byron played an outstanding game, stopping 90 per cent of the shots on his gate. His tenacity, pluck, and sheer ability should be an inspiration to all of you in future games."

With that, Maxwell walked out of the dressing room, slamming the door behind him.

*F*rank was troubled by the outcome of the game against Selkirk. He left the Amphitheatre alone, needing time to think. He knew the Falcons were a good team and yet, as Coach Maxwell had pointed out, they were still playing as individuals. As team captain, Frank felt it was his responsibility to find a way to weld the Falcons into a cohesive unit.

Walking on Broadway, he was hailed by a young woman crossing the intersection at Osborne and Broadway.

"Good evening, Frank," she called. "Returning home from hockey practice?"

Frank was delighted and a little embarrassed to see Bea Peterson. He'd been too busy to ask her to dinner.

"Hello, Bea. I'm returning from a disappointing game. What brings you out on such a miserable December night?"

"I'm on my way home from the Fort Garry Hotel. I play piano in the lounge."

They walked on in silence, passing the spacious home of Thomas Robertson, a coal merchant and a staunch supporter of Winnipeg's hockey combine. Frank thought the house's somber granite façade looked as cold and stern as a stone pulpit.

"Do they pay well at the Fort Garry?"

"They pay a pittance. But it's good practice and the audience appreciates the classics. I haven't given up my dream of becoming a concert pianist," Bea replied. "Why don't you give up that silly boy's game of hockey and take up the violin again? You showed great promise."

Frank was only half listening to Bea. He was focused on her comment about having a dream. As long as he had known Bea, she had pursued her career as a musician. He knew it hadn't been easy for her. Though she was talented, her parents did not have the resources to send her to a school like the Toronto Conservatory which would have opened doors for Bea. And yet, thought Frank, she persevered and never complained, practicing by day and working by night.

"It must be wonderful to have a dream," said Frank.

"Don't you have one, Frank?"

"No, not really. I've always wanted to be good at something, like hockey or music, but I've never completely focused on either. I've never dreamed of becoming the very best in my chosen field. For that matter, I don't have a chosen field. I like hockey and I enjoyed music, until Sarah passed away. I haven't played the violin since."

Bea looked up at the clear winter sky. The constellations blazed like diamonds strung on fine-braid wire.

"A person without a dream is the saddest creature on earth. For without a dream, he can never realize his true destiny. At the end of the day, he'll look back and wonder if he chose the correct path, the path God intended for him."

"I have forsaken my belief in God," he said.

"Then you are condemned to follow myriad paths, none of which will lead to your true fate because God and the dream are one and the same," said Bea.

Frank looked at her incredulously.

"You're talking gibberish, Bea."

"Perhaps," she retorted. "But it's what your sister believed."

"How would you know what she believed?" he shot back.

"I was beside her at her deathbed. She told me she would die in peace knowing that her role in this life was fulfilled."

"By her role, I assume you refer to her dream," said Frank with contempt.

"That's exactly what I mean, and what she meant," said Bea who stopped, angry at Frank.

"Bea, my sister was in her mid-20s when she died. She wasn't old enough to know her purpose in life, let alone fulfill it!" Frank glowered at the young woman.

Bea turned her face away and marched forward.

"You're wrong. Your sister's dream was to share her gift of music with others. She did it admirably and selflessly. How many people have you inspired, Frank? You're ego is so large I'm surprised you notice that lesser beings actually exist in this world."

"How dare you accuse me of hubris. I've fought for my country, stood by my family, and…"

"And what, Frank? You're nearly 25 and you're still playing a stupid boy's game. Why is that? So you can be the center, the captain, the hero? I'm sure all the women fall into a titter when the great Frank Fredrickson skates by."

"So that's it. You're angry because women find me attractive and I haven't called to ask you to dinner."

Bea turned to confront him again. "That's so typical. It's always about you, isn't it?"

Frank halted in mid-stride.

Bea continued. "When you arrived back in Winnipeg last spring, what was your first thought when you jumped from the train? Was it for your sister who loved you? Or was it for that ridiculous mob of hockey players who adore you?"

"How can you be so cruel, Bea? How can you question my love for my sister?"

"I'm not. I know you loved Sarah, but I think you love yourself more."

Frank passed Bea and walked on alone.

"Do you know what else Sarah said to me before she died?" Bea called after him.

Frank ignored her, forging ahead by himself over the hard-packed snow.

"She said I hope my brother Frank discovers his dream."

While he walked, Frank thought of another experience overseas he would never share with Bea.

In the summer of 1918 in Scotland he had met a beautiful young woman, a gifted musician who reminded him very much of Bea and his sister Sarah. Her name was Faith Laidlay, the only daughter of a wealthy Scottish family. Frank had fallen in love with Faith. When he was with her, the deep ache he felt at the loss of his beloved sister and the separation from his family and friends in Winnipeg abated. He sang with Faith when she played the violin or the piano. They attended operas in Edinburgh and danced together at balls at the Laidlay manor. Faith was the salve that soothed Frank's broken heart over the loss of Sarah. Faith was the one person who prevented him from spiraling into depression when he thought of Sarah.

In his first clumsy attempt to impress Faith, he flew his plane over the Laidlay estate, performed a barrel roll and lost control of the aircraft. He crash landed on the Laidlays' golf course in the midst of a match between Faith's father, John Laidlay, and wealthy London clients. He was pulled from the wreckage by Mr. Laidlay and his guests and spent the next month in hospital recovering from his wounds. Faith visited often, the bond between them grew and they professed their mutual love. They decided to marry. And then Faith was wrenched out of his life as quickly and brutally as Sarah had been. One lovely April day, he called at the Laidlay mansion to ask Faith out for a stroll. He was received at the door by Faith's father who handed him a terse note:

> "My daughter has told me of what has happened with regard to you and her. It is a proposition I could never consent to. There are many reasons for coming to this conclusion.
>
> I am very sorry it should have happened, but now that it has, the best and only thing to do is not to come near here or see her again."
>
> Yours truly,
>
> J.M. Laidlay

Discrimination, thought Frank, was not just reserved for the British establishment in Winnipeg. Apparently, the entire world was composed of bigots. He was crushed by the loss of Faith. But the episode had kindled a callus desire on his part to stand up to the world, to make a name for himself, to do something so heroic that no one would ever again consider Frank and his people worthless. He had never thought it a dream, only a revenge.

CHAPTER TWENTY-FIVE

The players in the dressing room fell silent as Frank entered. The teammates had been advised by Coach Maxwell that their captain had something important to say before their game against Brandon. For the first time in their careers, all the players were dressed in similar uniforms: green, gold and brown striped turtleneck sweaters and socks, with Falcon in bright orange lettering on the front of the jerseys. The new attire was courtesy of Billy Finlay and the senior members of Laycock & Company who had contributed a hundred dollars apiece to outfit the boys in the uniforms.

"Gentlemen," said Frank, casting his eye about the room. "In your sartorial splendor, I hardly recognize you. Perhaps clothes really do make the man."

There was laughter when Goodman suggested that the females in the crowd would now find the Falcons completely irresistible.

"I want to speak to you about something of importance to all of us," Frank continued. "A friend suggested to me recently that we all need a goal in life, something to strive for, something to motivate us, something to drive us forward against the most unlikely odds.

"What we require, gentlemen, is a dream, a dream of such power, and triumph, and glory that it would seem impossible to achieve. This, gentlemen, is about realizing our full potential as teammates and human beings."

There was some whispering among the Falcons. Most had never looked beyond winning the Manitoba League title. The idea of a much bigger world of hockey had never occurred to them.

"As individuals," continued Frank, "we are talented hockey players.

But as a team we still have not developed the spirit, cohesiveness, and unselfishness required of champions."

Friddy objected to the remark.

"We're as good a team as any."

"If we're such a good team, why did Selkirk beat us last week?" retorted Frank.

Friddy didn't reply.

"They beat us because they have a dream, a dream about winning the Allan Cup. They won it in 1916 as the 61st Battalion and they're determined to win it again this season. They play with spirit and cohesiveness because they're not afraid to look to the future."

"What's our goal to be then, Frank?" asked Friddy. "To become hockey champions of the world?"

There was laughter in the dressing room.

"Yes!" said Frank. "That's exactly it. And not so far-fetched because hockey will be included as a sport for the first time this year at the Olympic Games in Antwerp. The winner of the Allan Cup will represent Canada."

The Falcons looked at each other. Was their captain joking? How could a group of Icelandic immigrants who had learned to skate on backyard ponds hope to capture a Holy Grail such as an Olympic gold medal? They had been made to feel inferior by the ruling class for so long that they lacked true self-confidence. They knew they were good fundamental hockey players, but at a deeper level they really didn't believe in themselves as a hockey team. That rejection had little by little, year after year, eroded their spirits, and washed away the fighting instinct that characterized their forebears. To an extent they had become like rudderless ships on a great ocean with no land or hope in sight. Now their captain was giving them something to strive for, to dream about, a shining disc of gold just discernible on the edge of the horizon. And all they needed to do to succeed was to struggle together like a crew of Vikings.

Slim stood. "I like the dream, Frankie."

"So do I," said Konnie.

"Me too," said Wally.

"You can count on me, Frank," said Bobby.

"Ditto for me," said Mike.

"To win an Olympic medal would suit me just fine," said Woodman.

The last man to stand was Friddy.

"I think we're a damn fine team without this dream," he said. "But I suppose it can't hurt. Now let's go out and show Brandon what we've got!"

Falcon Squad Shows Spirit and Discipline
By Billy Finlay

Team spirit and solidarity are chiefly responsible for the wonderful success the Falcon hockey club has enjoyed since a disappointing loss early in the season to their old nemesis, the Selkirk Fishermen. The Icelanders, showing exceptional discipline on the ice, hammered Brandon 9-2 on Sunday. Frank Fredrickson and his teammates face the greatest challenge of their Cinderella season tomorrow night when they once again face off against the powerful Selkirk Fishermen at the Amphitheatre. The game is pivotal as a win for either team will guarantee a first-place finish in the Manitoba Hockey League and an opportunity to challenge the winner of the City League for a chance to make an appearance in the Western Cup Final. Local pucksters can rest assured that the Fishermen, led by Crutchy Morrison and Bullet Joe Simpson, will not easily be denied a berth in the final against the City League champ. This will be the most exciting match of the season! Hang onto your hats and arrive early if you want a ticket.

CHAPTER TWENTY-SIX

*E*xcitement hung in the frigid air. The line of hockey fans snaked from the entrance of the Amphitheatre four blocks to the corner of Broadway and Spence. Some had waited all night in 25 below zero weather to purchase tickets while scalpers worked the crowd mercilessly getting $20 for a $1 ticket.

Inside the Amphitheatre's press booth, Billy Finlay lit a Pathfinder cigar and checked his phone connection to the Free Press editorial department.

"Pond, is that you?" Finlay clicked the receiver several times.

"Yes, sir, Billy, I'm here." The former copy boy had worked his way up to cub reporter in the sports department.

"Okay, Pond. Get ready. Have you got a spare pencil and lots of copy paper because I'm going to dictate the game to you play by play and I don't want you to miss a word."

"Yes sir, Billy."

From his vantage point, Finlay could see the Amphitheatre was in pandemonium. Jack Snidal, a long-time Falcons' fan, climbed onto a brass rail that ran along the top of the boards and attempted to navigate the slippery pipe like a tight-rope walker, arms outstretched for balance. When the 250-pound giant slipped after a few feet and crashed to the ice, a roar of approval went up from the crowd.

"Good old, Jack. He's a pisser," yelled one man, spitting his false teeth onto the ice in his excitement.

The Falcons, led by Frank, skated onto the ice to loud applause. Frank picked up the false teeth and handed them back to the man who rewarded him with a toothless smile.

The Falcons gathered around Wally at the goal to discuss their game plan one last time.

"Remember boys," said Frank, "Steamer wants us to play a defensive first period. We'll only rush two men and keep the rest back."

The bell rang to open the first period and the teams lined up at center. Frank surveyed the opposition as he prepared to take the face-off against Crutchy Morrison. The Fishermen looked to be in top condition. Frank noted that their star defenseman, Bullet Joe Simpson, had "the stare": a gleam in his eye that indicated he was on his game, ready to take the opposition apart.

Frank won the face-off and flipped the puck over to Slim on the right wing who carried the puck deep into the Fishermen's scoring zone. When Slim attempted to center the puck, Bullet Joe intercepted the pass and began a blistering rush up the ice. It was only the speed and back checking skills of Goodman that prevented Bullet from completing his rush and taking a shot on net. Goodman carried the puck back down the left wing into the Fishermen's corner where defenseman Rube Brandow slammed him into the boards from behind. A cry of disapproval erupted from the partisan Falcons crowd. But the play continued with Brandow stripping the puck from Goodman, passing it across ice to his defensive partner, Bullet Simpson. This time the swift defenseman was unstoppable. He weaved his way down ice outmaneuvering Frank and the rest of the Falcons to rip a shot into the top corner of the net.

"I should have stopped that!" Wally said as his teammates lined up at center for the face-off.

In the press box, Billy Finlay relayed the news to Pond.

"Simpson has scored the opener at 4:15 of the first. Have you got that?"

"Yes, Billy."

In the crowd, Mac MacPherson smiled smugly.

"I told you they were nothing but ne'er-do-well immigrants," he said to his son.

A few seats to the back of MacPherson, sat the senior partners of Laycock & Company.

"I'll wager a fiver that the Falcons will score the next goal," Laycock said to MacPherson.

"Add a fiver for me," said Solmundson.

"And also for me," said Levine.

"I'll take some of that action myself," said Minnie. "How about you, Haldora?"

"Count me in."

"Do you people like to lose money?" smirked MacPherson.

Frank lost the face-off to Morrison who flipped the puck into the Falcons' end. Pete Mitchell, fed a pass by Jocko Anderson, drove hard to the net and nearly scored on a backhand shot that Wally caught and held with the edge of his glove. As play continued, the Fishermen were relentless. They fired a barrage of shots at Wally, who used every part of his body to prevent the opposition from scoring a second goal. The Fishermen's defensemen pinched in deep, the entire team swarmed around the Falcons' net. Frank, fighting for control of the puck in front of his goal, poked it away from Morrison. The puck was picked up by Slim. He broke away and zigzagged around Brandow, the lone defenseman. Slim's shot was hard and accurate and found its way between the goaltender's legs.

A triumphant cry arose from the throng in the Amphitheatre.

"Halderson, Halderson!"

While Jack Snidal made a second attempt at walking the brass rail, Finlay was on the line to Pond.

"Halderson has tied it at 10:05. Have you got that?"

"Yes, sir. It sounds as if you've got a grand game in progress. Would you like me to join you?"

"Hell no, Pond. Just continue to take copy."

Laycock looked at MacPherson.

"Should I collect our winnings now or would you like to make a further wager on the outcome of the game?" he asked

MacPherson refused to acknowledge Laycock. The big man was calculating sums in his head. After a pause, he said:

"I'll bet $10,000 on Selkirk to win."

Laycock was stunned. It was a fortune, more than his law firm and his ranch north of Winnipeg were worth. If he were to lose the bet, everything he had worked for, indeed, everything he and his partners had worked for, would be forfeited to MacPherson. He was about to refuse when Minnie leaned toward him.

"I'll take half that action."

"Are you absolutely sure?" asked Laycock.

"Do I look like a gal who would kid you?"

Laycock smiled.

"Okay, MacPherson," he said. "You're on."

The second period started with a powerful offense by the Fishermen. Bullet Joe, Crutchy Morrison, and Jocko Anderson attempted rush after rush at the Falcons' goal, only to be turned back by a swarming defense and Wally's determined goaltending. By mid-period both teams were exhausted and the game seemed at a standstill. But then Crutchy Morrison broke lose and placed a neat wrist shot between Wally's legs. Inspired by his teammate's effort, Pete Mitchell caromed a shot off Frank's skate, scoring another goal for the Fishermen. Ten seconds later, Jocko Anderson took a pass from Mitchell and scored another marker for the powerful Selkirk team.

"I hope you are good for your $10,000 bet, Mr. Laycock," beamed MacPherson.

Laycock stared at the ice and said nothing.

The teams lined up for the face-off at center ice. Frank won the draw and fired the puck across to Slim who carried it into the Selkirk zone and ripped a shot off the crossbar. Crutchy Morrison picked up the puck and corkscrewed his way down the ice, passing the puck at the last minute to Ernie Anderson who backhanded a shot into the left corner of the Falcons' net. The score was 5-1.

MacPherson was jubilant. He stood up and applauded Anderson's goal.

"Well, Laycock," he said. "Would you like to up our little wager?"

Laycock and his partners stared at each other. With the Falcons facing a four-goal deficit, the odds of them coming back were slender. The senior partners huddled together with Minnie and Haldora. It took a long time to reach a decision. Minnie finally persuaded the group.

"We'll not only meet the $10,000," announced Laycock, "but we're ready to double the bet."

MacPherson threw back his head and guffawed.

"Done," he said.

As the last minutes of the second period ticked away, Steamer substituted Friddy for an exhausted Goodman.

Frank won the face-off and passed the puck to Friddy on the left wing. With his fresh legs pumping hard, Friddy penetrated the Fishermen's scoring zone before he could be back checked. Using his speed and strength, he split the defense of Bullet Joe and Brandow and rushed in alone on net. He beat Bobby Morrison with a subtle wrist shot that skipped across the ice and jumped over the goalie's stick.

The Falcon supporters cheered as the bell rang to end the second period. But Friddy's goal seemed too little too late. With only 20 minutes left to play, how could the Falcons come back from a 5-2 deficit against a powerful team like the Fishermen?

MacPherson turned and glared at Laycock and his colleagues.

"I'll enjoy spending my $20,000," he said, leering at Haldora and Minnie.

CHAPTER TWENTY-SEVEN

*F*riddy's late goal had done little to inspire the Falcons. The dressing room was hushed as the teammates watched Steamer Maxwell pace the floor.

"What the hell's wrong with you? The Fishermen are making you look like tired old women! Are you all losers? Where's your pride, your honor, your team spirit?"

The teammates said nothing. Maxwell continued: "I agreed to coach this team because I believed in you. I thought you had guts, determination, the will to succeed. Yet all I see out there is a bunch of pathetic Goolies bent on self-destruction. I've got news. MacPherson is laughing at you chumps. He said you were ne'er-do-wells and now you're proving his point. No wonder they call you the team that nobody wants. I'm your coach and *I'm* sick of you. Well? Does one of you mewling sons of immigrants have anything to say?"

"I do."

It was Frank. He had remained standing throughout Maxwell's tirade.

"Enlighten me, Fredrickson. Tell me something I don't know."

"It's your fault we're losing this game," said Frank.

"My fault. MY FAULT!"

"Yes," said Frank, who stood his ground.

"And just how do you figure that, *Captain* Fredrickson?"

"You keep telling us to play defensively. But that's not our style. We're fighters, not defenders."

"Do you know why I tell you to play defensively, Fredrickson?"

"Yes."

"Enlighten me again, *Captain*."

"Because you don't believe in us any more than MacPherson and the rest believe. You think we're just a bunch of talentless backyard amateurs."

Steamer thought hard before he answered:

"You are a bunch of backyard amateurs... *but you are not without skills!* Just once—for my sake at least—put it all together. You had a good season this year. But never once did I see you play to your full potential. The Fishermen are a great team, probably the greatest team you'll ever face. You know why? Because they always give all they've got. I still haven't seen that spark of greatness in you. I've detected moments of brilliance. But you've never shown me sustained genius on the ice. Now would be a good time. Please give me something to believe in!"

Maxwell left the room, closing the door quietly behind him.

Frank removed the gold amulet with the embossed Viking warrior from around his neck. He held it in his hands as he faced his teammates.

"What's our dream?" he asked.

No one answered.

"What's our dream?" Frank asked again.

Bobby spoke up.

"To become the greatest hockey team in the world, although it would seem unlikely at this point."

There was some weak laughter from the rest of the teammates.

"What's our dream?" Frank asked again.

"To become the greatest team in the world." This time it was Konnie who answered. His deep baritone voice carried conviction.

"What's our dream?" asked Frank yet again.

"To become the best goddam hockey team in the whole bloody world," yelled Slim.

"Right," said Frank. Now let me hear you say it as if you mean it."

The Falcons got up and formed a circle around their captain, placing their hands over the amulet.

"What's our dream?" asked their captain.

"To become the greatest, most renowned, most beloved bunch of hockey stars in God's universe!"

Frank slipped the amulet back around his neck.

"Okay, gentlemen, let's show the world who we are."

CHAPTER TWENTY-EIGHT

*T*he crowd roared as the Falcons returned to the ice for the third period.

"Losers," screamed MacPherson and his son Fat Mac Jr.

"C'mon, Falcons. It's not over yet," hollered the members of Laycock & Co.

Billy Finlay was relaying copy to Pond on the phone.

"Standby, Pond," he said. "Here come the Falcons."

"How do they look, Billy?" asked Pond.

Finlay scanned the players as they skated around the rink.

"They aren't smiling, but they sure look determined. I wonder what was said in the dressing room?"

On the ice, Frank called a team meeting around Wally's net. He showed his teammates a note from Steamer:

"Forget the defensive game. Show me what you are really capable of. I believe."

Frank won the face-off and flipped the black disc to Mike. He carried it down the left wing, only to be stopped by Bullet Joe who began his own rush into the Falcons' zone. Goodman back checked ferociously, managing to strip the puck from Bullet and pass it across to Bobby. The short, powerful defenseman made a charge down the left wing, faking a pass to Frank who stood in front of the net tying up Brandow. Circling behind the goal, Bobby slammed the puck into the corner before the Selkirk goalie had time to move to the other side.

The reaction from the partisan crowd was immediate.

"Falcons, Falcons, Falcons!"

"I believe that's one for our side," said Laycock to MacPherson.

"One isn't enough. Your team doesn't have the heart to win this match."

At the face-off, the puck caromed off Frank's skate and was picked up by Crutchy Morrison who corkscrewed his way into the Falcons' end, ripping a high shot at Wally. The puck smacked him over his left eye. He dropped to the ice and the referee rang the bell for a time out. The Falcons skated around their fallen goalie. Frank helped Wally to his feet and examined the cut.

"That's a nasty gash," he said. "You may be out of the game."

"I don't care how bad it is, Frank. I'm not quitting."

The Falcons' assistant coach and trainer, Gudmundur Sigurjonsson, arrived at the net and examined the cut.

"You need stitches," said Sigurjonsson.

He motioned to the bench to send in Babe Elliot, the backup goalie.

"I'm not leaving the ice," said Wally. "Patch me up here."

Sigurjonsson considered. The cut was deep, but he could temporarily draw it together with a dressing. It would be tragic to lose Wally at this point in the game.

"Okay," said the trainer. "But if you feel faint get out of the game. You won't help the team by attempting to be a hero."

When play resumed with a face-off in the Falcons' end, Frank lost the draw to Crutchy who slammed a shot at Wally from 10 feet out. The goalie caught the puck with his glove. He dropped it behind the net where Bobby picked it up and carried it into the Fishermen's zone. His shot was blocked by Jocko Anderson. Anderson moved the puck across ice to Pete Mitchell who was back checked by Goodman. Goodman, on fire, was skating as fast backwards as forwards. He carried the puck down the ice and backhanded a shot at the Fishermen's goalie. The puck almost sailed over Morrison's shoulder before he stopped it with his face. The rebound was scooped up by Harry Oliver. He rushed into the Falcons' zone and blasted the puck straight at Wally's groin. The beleaguered goalie dropped to the ice, smothering the rebound.

The face-off was in the Falcons' zone to the right of Wally. It was won by Crutchy and passed to Bullet Simpson. Before he could unleash a shot, Simpson was back checked by Goodman. Mike flipped the disc to

Frank at center. He zigzagged around Crutchy, stick handling the puck into the Fishermen's zone. He dropped the puck for Slim, following the play. The lanky winger carried it into the corner. Fighting off a check from Simpson, Slim centered the puck to Frank. He was knocked flat by Brandow. From the ground, Frank used his stick to slide the disc to Slim, charging the net. Taking the pass on his backhand, Slim slipped a shot between the goalie's legs.

"Teamwork, Falcons. Teamwork!" Thousands of voices cheered the team.

Other fans yelled: "Speed, Falcons. Speed!"

With less than two minutes in regulation time, the Falcons were within one goal of tying the game and forcing overtime.

At center ice, Crutchy won the draw and passed the puck back to Bullet Joe. The explosive defenseman stick handled through the Falcons before Goodman could catch him from behind. Simpson managed to unleash a blistering shot that hit the crossbar. The rebound dropped in front of Wally where a mass of players fought to get control of the puck. Johannesson finally succeeded. With 15 seconds left in the game, he began a rush up the ice. The Fishermen were caught behind the play. Spotting Goodman on right wing, Johannesson passed the disc across to the faster skater. Goodman took the pass on the fly and began a last desperate sprint into the Fishermen's zone. Bullet Joe tried to catch up but Goodman had a clear breakaway. Faking a forehand shot, Goodman switched to his backhand and lofted the puck over the goalie's shoulder into the net.

A riot broke out in the Amphitheatre. Unbelievably, the Falcons had come back from a three-goal deficit to tie the match at 5-5. Even the most sedate fans climbed onto their seats and roared their approval at the tying marker. The group from Laycock & Company hugged each other; Mr. Levine shocked his colleagues by removing his shirt and throwing it onto the ice.

Laycock couldn't resist a barb at MacPherson. "I believe the game is tied and the momentum is in our favor."

MacPherson did not reply. He sat slumped in his seat playing with his diamond ring. He turned to look at Laycock. MacPherson's eyes burned like lignite. "Listen sonny, Mac MacPherson has never lost a bet in his life. And this game is going into overtime. I'll expect payment of our $20,000 wager in cash in my office first thing tomorrow morning."

CHAPTER TWENTY-NINE

*T*here was a short intermission while the exhausted teams prepared for sudden death overtime. The Falcons remained on the players' bench with Coach Maxwell.

"Whatever the outcome of this game, I'm proud of you boys," said Steamer. "You just played the best damn hockey I've witnessed in my career as player or coach."

"Of course we did," quipped Bobby. "We're the best team in the world."

"That's what I call confidence," laughed Frank as the bell rang to signal the beginning of overtime.

Jocko Anderson scooped up the puck at the face-off, and rushed at the Falcons' goal, crashing into Wally but failing to put the disc in the net. Bobby lifted the puck down the ice where Bullet Joe took control, stick handling to center ice before he was back checked by Goodman. After that, the play became ragged with neither team able to mount a convincing offense. At the end of the first overtime, the shots on goal were eight for the Fishermen and none for the Falcons.

Back on the bench, the teammates leaned against each other for support. They had pushed themselves beyond physical and mental endurance. What did they have left?

"You have heart," said Steamer, reading their minds. "The team with the most heart is going to win this game. True champions always have it. You've shown me that you've got everything else. Now get out there and show me you've got what it takes to finish this game!"

The puck was fired into the Falcons' zone from the face-off. The Fishermen took advantage by rushing their forwards and defensemen deep into scoring position. Using the last of their endurance, the Fishermen fired a volley of shots at Wally who was having difficulty controlling the rebounds. Charging the net, Bullet Joe one-timed a rebound that hit the goal post. It would have been in the net if Konnie had not deflected it with his stick. Rallying the Falcons, the big defenseman moved down center ice taking two Selkirk players to the ice with him. His rush was stopped by Mitchell. He raced down the wing and fed Brandow a pass in front of the Falcon goal. Byron made a brilliant save with an outstretched glove and flipped the puck to Bobby. He corkscrewed down the ice, taking a sizzling shot at Morrison. The goalie made the save but couldn't stop the rebound. Slim, following the play, flicked the bouncing disc into the net for the winning goal.

A riot broke out in the Amphitheatre. Fans leaped over the boards and swarmed onto the ice to congratulate the Falcons.

In the press booth, Billy Finlay, hardly able to breathe from excitement, did his best to describe to Pond the last minutes of the game and the pandemonium that ensued.

"You'd better get every word of this Pond," Finlay threatened. "This is the best hockey that Winnipeg has ever witnessed, perhaps ever will witness."

In the stands, the supporters from Laycock & Company gathered together. Haldora and Minnie cried, while the senior partners threw their hats in the air and slapped each other on the back. When Laycock finally looked for MacPherson, he saw the man slipping out an exit.

"MacPherson! I believe we have a small wager to settle."

"You'll get your damn money when I'm good and ready to pay," MacPherson retorted.

"I hope that's soon," said Laycock, "because I wouldn't want it to get around Winnipeg that Mac MacPherson welshes on his gambling debts."

When the Falcons were finally able to disengage themselves from their admirers and make their way back to their dressing room, Billy Finlay squeezed into the room with them.

"Congratulations, lads," said Finlay, handing out Cuban cigars.

"Have you heard what the City League executive is saying about your victory?"

Every ear was suddenly tuned to Finlay.

"They're saying the Fishermen are a weak team that could have been trounced by any City League squad."

"Those bastards will never give us our due," said Slim in disgust.

"Don't worry," said Frank. "We'll find out who the better team is when we play the City League's champion."

CHAPTER THIRTY

*S*lim barged through the door of the Falcons' dressing room brandishing a roster of players for the Winnipeg Winnipegs, the winner of the City League. Tickets for the two-game championship between the Manitoba League and the Winnipeg League had been sold out a week before the first game.

"Take a look at this, boys," Slim said. "Fat Mac Jr. is playing defense for the Winnipegs."

The teammates gathered round Slim to check the line-up.

"It looks as if Fat Mac Sr. has pulled a few strings to get his son on the team," said Bobby. "Wasn't Junior Mac playing intermediate hockey for the Monarchs this season?"

"Yeh, and he warmed the bench with his big arse," said Mike.

"It seems we have an opportunity for a little payback," said Konnie. "What do you think, Frank?"

Fredrickson leaned against a cinder block wall. Fat Mac Jr., he thought, was one of the dirtiest, most undisciplined players in local hockey. He had injured many first-rate players including Steamer Maxwell. And Frank would never forget the personal score he himself had to settle with the malicious lout.

"We don't want to jeopardize the game for the sake of revenge, but if we catch Mac Jr. skating with his head down, we might just give him a gentle reminder to keep his head up," said Frank.

"He always skates with his head down," said Friddy.

Frank looked at Friddy and winked.

Up in the press box, Billy Finlay lit a cigarette, took a swig of Canadian Club from his flask, and checked the phone connection to the Free Press.

"Are you ready, Pond?"

"Oh, yes sir, Billy. Ready as the Bard himself."

Laycock looked about for Mac MacPherson. The city's richest man was always the last to arrive so he and his wife could make an impressive entrance in their latest finery. A minute before game time, MacPherson waddled down the stairs in what looked like a $200 suit; his wife's dress was simple yet elegant and her necklace blazed with diamonds. Laycock also noted that Fat Mac Sr. smiled benevolently on all the lesser folk. The man seemed in a grand mood. He was, after all, about to witness the triumph of the City League over the Icelanders.

"MacPherson," called Laycock. "It appears your bank draft for $20,000 has become lost in the mail. It hasn't arrived and our wager was weeks ago."

A scowl replaced the rigid smile on MacPherson's countenance.

"I told you to expect your money when I felt like sending it," said MacPherson.

"Are you telling me that Mac MacPherson isn't good for it?" asked Laycock as loudly as possible.

"Quiet!" yelled MacPherson. "You'll have your filthy cash tomorrow morning."

Then a greedy smile embossed his face. "Unless you'd like to double our wager on the outcome of tonight's game?"

"Why should I make a further bet with a man who doesn't pay his debts?" said Laycock.

"Because I have your money with me now." MacPherson flourished a draft for $20,000 made out to Laycock & Company.

Laycock was taken aback.

"I'll confer with my colleagues."

Laycock, Solmundson, Levine, Haldora and Minnie discussed the proposal.

"I can't afford to cover a wager like that," said Haldora.

"We don't expect you to," said Laycock. "You'll only cover what you can afford."

Levine and Solmundson were also reluctant. It was a staggering sum. If they were to lose, they would be in debt for the rest of their lives.

It was Minnie who again took the initiative.

"What's the matter with you people? Do we believe in the Falcons or not? Have they let us down yet? Let's show some confidence in the Icelanders. Let's take this buffoon's bet. It's like money in the bank."

"Okay," said Laycock after more consideration. "We'll do it. All agreed?"

Everyone raised a hand to indicate yes. Laycock's voice quavered as he accepted MacPherson's wager.

"Capital, old boy," said MacPherson. "And just to show my good faith I'll let you hold this draft for $20,000."

Laycock took the check and folded it carefully inside the pocket of his suit.

At the face-off, Frank stole the puck from Winnipegs' center Jimmy Gibson. He rushed hard into the scoring zone, passing the puck to Slim on right wing. Frank continued to bear down on Bill Binney, the goalie. Slim flipped the puck behind the net to Mike on right wing. Goodman danced around defenseman Moose Moran, centering the puck to Frank who one-timed the disc between Binney's legs.

There was a burst of applause from the Falcons' supporters.

"I believe that's a marker for our team," Laycock called to MacPherson over the din.

Before the game resumed, Fat Mac Jr. was substituted for Moose Moran at defense.

Frank won the draw again and flipped the puck back to Konnie on defense. The big man began a rush that was broken up by Red Dutton, the Winnipegs' star defenseman. Dutton passed the puck to Mac Jr. who slashed at Slim's ankles in an attempt to get the puck out of the Winnipegs' zone. It was a costly mistake because Mac's head was down, allowing Slim to catch him with a vicious shoulder check. The defenseman hit the boards so hard that his suspenders broke and his hockey pants slid down to his ankles as he got to his feet. There was delighted applause from the crowd.

"You're a disgrace to the MacPherson name!" yelled Mac Sr. from the stands.

The game continued with the Falcons firmly in control. Goodman scored on a backhand shot from a face-off in the Winnipegs' zone. This was followed by a rifle shot by Frank from 10 feet out, which the goalie never saw until it was in the mesh at the back of the net. Then Woodman, substituting for Goodman who had been injured when Mac Jr. had cross-checked him in the corner, blasted a shot from the far left wing that found its mark in the top corner of the net. When the bell rang to end the first period, the score was 3-0 in favor of the Falcons.

In the press box, Finlay relayed copy to Pond.

"I don't know why this MacPherson Jr. hasn't received a penalty," said Finlay. "If he's not hooking, he's cross checking or slashing. Makes me think someone paid the ref to ignore his cheating."

In the stands, Laycock and his colleagues prayed the Falcons' three-goal lead would hold up.

Frank easily won the draw at the start of the second period, charged down the ice, and split the defense. He beat Binney with a beautiful wrist shot that caromed into the net off the goalie's skate. He turned, holding up his stick in a victory salute. Fat Mac Jr. rammed his stick into Frank's chest. The Icelander's captain dropped to the ice.

"This doesn't look good," said Finlay to Pond. "MacPherson has illegally checked Fredrickson who remains prone on the ice."

The Falcons' trainer rushed onto the ice while Frank's teammates formed a protective circle around their fallen leader.

"Damn Goolie deserved a good hit. Can't take the rough stuff," said Mac Jr. as the ref finally called a penalty.

Slim skated to the penalty box and warned Mac Jr. to keep his eyes open.

"Screw you, Goolie!" screamed MacPherson, glaring at Slim through little pig eyes.

Frank recovered quickly with smelling salts under his nose.

"I'm okay. Just a little winded," he said as his teammates hauled him to his feet.

The referee called a short rest period for Frank to clear his head.

When the bell rang to resume play, Frank won the draw, passing the disc back to Bobby. He began a blitz down the left wing. Entering the scoring zone, he dropped the puck for Mike. He stick handled into the corner, fought off the Winnipegs' defenseman, and centered the puck to Frank. He deflected the disc into the goal with the tip of his stick.

The Falcons' supporters were ecstatic. With a 5-0 lead and only a few minutes left in the game the outcome seemed beyond doubt.

"Would you care to increase our bet?" Laycock asked casually of MacPherson.

There was no answer.

The game resumed. Frank fought for the puck and passed it to Slim who carried the disc into the right corner. Instead of charging to the net, Frank held back, waiting along the right wing boards. MacPherson, his penalty served, lumbered into the corner to battle Slim for the puck. The deft stick handler allowed MacPherson to strip the puck from him without a fight.

"I could swear Halderson gave that puck away on purpose," said a perplexed Finlay to Pond.

MacPherson began a clumsy rush up the ice with his head down. He did not see Frank coming at him full speed from the opposite direction. The collision was like a locomotive running into a fattened cow. MacPherson cleared the boards, landing ass first on his mother and father who were in the first row of seats. Mac Sr. and his wife fought to extricate themselves while the audience roared. The laughter did not abate until the couple, followed by their son, left the arena.

Falcons Capture Manitoba Honors
*Icelanders Swamp 'Pegs in Second Game, Win Series and
Provincial Championship*

By Billy Finlay

The Falcons will represent Manitoba in the play-downs for
the Allan Cup and the right to compete in the Olympic Games
at Antwerp for the world's hockey championship. This was
determined at the Amphitheatre rink last evening when
the speedy Icelanders, traveling at the same dizzy clip that
has taken them through to a remarkable season of victories,
skipped over a 10 to 1 victory on the Winnipegs in the second
and final game of the provincial title play-off, winning the
series and the championship by the score of 15 goals to 1.
The performance of the Falcons was well nigh faultless and
the ease with which the champions romped away with the
game established beyond any shadow of a doubt the marked
superiority of the Manitoba leaguers...

The Falcons' next opponent is Fort William in the Western
Hockey Final.

Falcons Advance to Allan Cup Final against University of Toronto Blue and White
Icelandic Brigade Dumps Fort William in Two-Game Playoff

By Billy Finlay

The Falcons out-skated and out-shot Fort William to win the two-game playoff in the Western Allan Cup final with ease in front of 4,500 home town fans at the Amphitheatre on Wednesday night. A barrage of shots on the opponents' citadel by Fredrickson, Halderson and Goodman kept the Fort William boys busy in their own end attempting to clear the puck for a good part of each match. The final score for the lightning fast Falcons who never looked ruffled was 16 to 3 for the series, tallying 7 markers to Fort William's 2 in the first game, and 9 markers to Fort William's 1 in the second...

———•◦•———

Trip to Allan Cup Reward for Years of Hard Work
Local Boys Have Developed Into Champions After Overcoming Many Obstacles – Players Struggled For Many Years Before Achieving Honors

By Billy Finlay

The Falcon hockey club has been a growth and development, rather than a sudden creation. The team did not rise to the giddy heights of fame and notoriety in a day or in a season. Rather, its career from practical obscurity to a place in the full glare of the brightest limelight, has savored somewhat of a natural evolution from a chrysalis stage, gradual but sure. Its history, from its origin to its present position virtually at the pinnacle of Canadian amateur hockey, can almost be reckoned as one of the romances of the game in the Dominion. The triumph of the Falcons throughout the entire season has been the direct result of the intensive cultivation of team spirit and unity. Conjoined to the subtle connecting link that race and kindred make, came that other superimposed feeling of fellowship born together in the army...

The players have been together in the game practically from infancy. They went through the mill together in the old Independent League days, and after seeing service overseas, decided to stick together through thick and thin, and make a bid for entrance into the senior City League. They found their path beset with obstacles, and finally, after a storm of controversy, while unable to burst the old combine that holds sway in the city, they managed, by effecting an alliance with Selkirk and Brandon, to form a new league of equal rank with the existing Winnipeg League...

To say the Icelanders are the pride of Winnipeg hockey fandom is putting it mildly, and the boys are happy to think they are going to have an opportunity of bringing the Allan Cup back to Winnipeg. Well, here's good luck to you, boys.

CHAPTER THIRTY-TWO

Toronto, March 28, 1920

*T*he Toronto press was abuzz with excitement. Stories comparing the merits of the University of Toronto Varsity team, the eastern representative in the Allan Cup, with those of the Winnipeg Falcons filled the sports pages. Because Eastern Canada believed it owned the cup, Toronto sports reporters thought the Falcons were hopelessly outmatched by the Varsity Blue and White.

"What we have here," wrote one reporter, "is a gang of rural upstarts contemplating victory over one of Eastern Canada's most talented hockey squads. Man for man the Toronto Varsity squad is superior to the Falcons at every position. It might do well for the Falcons to forfeit the series now, return to their bucolic life in Winnipeg, and thereby avoid humiliation by the mighty Varsity team."

"What does bucolic mean?" asked Slim, as the Falcons got dressed in the locker room before the opening match of the two-game series.

"It means the arse who wrote that likely has never been farther west than Brampton," said Frank.

The Toronto Arena was filling to capacity. The start of the game had to be delayed as fans continued to jam into the rink. Some intrepid spectators, who held standing-room-only tickets and wanted a better view, climbed out on iron girders that spanned the rink high above the ice.

Led by goalie Jack Langtry, the Varsity squad skated onto the ice to a roar from the spectators. The Toronto teammates skated a circuit of the ice before they began to warm up Langtry with shots on his net. Minutes later the Falcons, led by Frank, skated onto the ice. A small contingent of fans from Manitoba raised a Falcons banner with the words "Speed Falcons, Speed!" The Manitobans' cheers could not be heard over the thunderous Varsity crowd

In the press box, Billy Finlay was connected to Winnipeg by telegraph. His rookie reporter, Alan Pond, stood in front of the Free Press building with a megaphone ready to announce the goals as they were scored.

Frank was pitted against team captain Bill Carson, a prolific goal scorer for the Varsity Blue and White. Carson won the draw and passed the rubber to his left-winger Roper Gouinlock. He sped down the ice and centered the puck in front of the net. Johannesson intercepted and moved the puck across ice to the fleet Benson, rushing into the Varsity zone. Benson was stopped by the Blue and White's right defenseman, Pete McIntyre. He lugged the puck along the boards but was flattened by Goodman. He fired a hard shot that hit the Blue's goal post. The rebound was scooped up by left defenseman Beattie Ramsay. Ramsay corkscrewed his way up center ice, making a brilliant charge that would have resulted in a goal if Byron hadn't deflected the rubber with his glove. The deflection was picked up by Fredrickson. Gathering speed, he outmaneuvered the entire Varsity team, scoring the first goal of the match with three minutes left in the opening period. His feat was countered seconds later by Gouinlock, scooping the puck into the net during a melee in front of the Falcons' net.

"Get this to Pond," shouted Finlay.

"Fredrickson scores opener at 17:00 followed at 17:08 by Gouinlock for Varsity."

Despite the cold weather, a huge crowd had gathered in front of the Free Press to hear the most up-to-date results of the game. A cheer arose from the throng when Fredrickson's goal was announced by Pond, followed by boos when Gouinlock's marker was broadcast.

The Toronto fans were confident that the Varsity Blue would crush the Icelanders in the second period. Six minutes into the period, Langtry caught and held a wicked blast from Halderson that resulted in a face-off to the left side of the Varsity goal. Winning the draw, Frank passed the puck to Goodman in the slot. He rifled a shot into the top corner of Langtry's citadel. Five minutes later, Goodman and Frank broke out of their own zone and worked the rubber down the ice with slick cross-ice passes. Goodman skated behind the Varsity's defense and Frank placed the disc perfectly on his stick. Mike ripped the puck into the net before Langtry had a chance to move.

Back in Winnipeg, the crowd in front of the Free Press building became more boisterous. The multitude of fans continued to increase with each Falcon goal and it became impossible for Pond to be heard through his megaphone. He resorted to writing the goals on a large blackboard.

The Blue and White refused to give up. They penetrated the Falcons' zone and unleashed a relentless attack that was finally broken up by the rugged teamwork of Konnie and Bobby. Joe Olson eventually broke through, blasting a wrist shot that Byron just managed to save. He dropped the puck to the side of the net where Frank picked it up, gained momentum, and stick handled through the entire Varsity team, scoring as he was upended at the last minute by defenseman Ramsay. Thirty seconds later Goodman scored on a long shot from center that hopped over the stick of the beleaguered Langtry.

Between the second and third periods, a group of Manitoba fans carrying the Falcons' banner decided to parade it around the ice. They didn't get far before a group of Varsity supporters attacked them, tearing the banner to shreds. A couple of stalwart Manitobans used the poles to beat off the angry Varsity fans. The episode might have escalated into a riot if the Toronto police had not been called in to break up the fracas.

At the beginning of the third period, Fredrickson and Halderson swooped down the ice together. Frank faked a pass to Slim which confused the defensemen. Using his break-away speed and adept stick handling, the Falcons' captain charged behind the defense and beat Langtry from a couple of feet out.

In the press booth, Finlay was so excited he was eating cigars instead of smoking them.

"Get this to Pond!"

"Fredrickson has scored his third goal of the game at 45 seconds into the third period. This match looks to be a runaway for the Icelanders."

But Varsity was tenacious. With five minutes left in the game, Gouinlock got a marker for the Blue and White when he beat Byron with a low shot to the corner.

Varsity won the face-off and Frank Sullivan carried the disc into the Falcons' zone, rifling a wrist shot at Byron who just managed to deflect it with his glove. Benson picked up the loose puck, making a determined sprint through the defenders with Frank on his right. Bobby placed a neat pass between the defenseman's legs and Frank one-timed the puck into the net for his fourth tally of the game.

"Fredrickson has scored his fourth of the night with minutes left in the match," crowed a triumphant Finlay.

Showing its indomitable spirit, Varsity scored seconds before the bell rang to end the contest. The score was 8-3. The Falcons appeared to have an invincible lead heading into the final match of the two-game Allan Cup series.

"*H*ey Frankie, take a gander at this." Slim entered Frank's hotel room and threw a copy of the Globe and Mail's sports section on his bed. A bold headline ran across the top of the page:

Falcons Greatest Allan Cup Team in Many Years
Toronto Scribe Hands Out Praise To Speedy Icelanders—Halderson, Fredrickson, And Goodman Best Forward Line Seen In Toronto In Years — Falcons Played Clean, Fast Games

A smaller story described the Falcons' 3-2 victory over Toronto Varsity in the second game of the Allan Cup final for an 11-5 sweep of the series.

"I'll be darned!" said Frank as he read the article. "We've worked so hard for this Slim, and yet I can hardly believe our dream has become a reality."

"It's not over, Frankie. We still have to win the Olympics and the Americans will be tough."

Frank lay back on his bed and thought about the upcoming international competition. Slim was right. Beating the U.S. was no foregone conclusion. He knew the American team included four expatriate Canadians, the hard-hitting McCormick brothers, Joe and Larry, who played their early hockey in Buckingham, Quebec, as well as Frank Red Synott of New Brunswick, and Herbert Drury of Ontario. The Yankee goaltender, Ray Bonney, had learned his hockey in Hull, Quebec.

Steamer Maxwell and the rest of the Falcons crowded into the room. Maxwell carried letters of introduction from Tommy Church, the mayor of Toronto.

Frank opened his letter which began:

To Whom It May Concern:

The bearer of this letter, whose signature is written in the margin for the purpose of identification, is Frank Fredrickson of the Falcon Hockey Club of the City of Winnipeg.

Mr. Fredrickson was born and educated in the City of Winnipeg and attended Kelvin Technical High School. He is twenty-five years of age, and resides at No. 603 Elgin Avenue. He is a member of the Falcon Hockey Club, Allan Cup Champions of Canada, and purposes visiting Belgium to attend the Olympic Games as a member of the Canadian Olympic Team. He is a young gentleman of good ability and excellent character, and in every way a sterling young Canadian.

Officials and others are requested to extend the usual courtesies, which will be reciprocated as occasion may afford opportunity.

Given under the Seal of the Corporation of the City of Toronto this thirty-first day of March, A.D. Nineteen hundred and twenty.

On the right side at the bottom, the document was signed by Mayor Church and the City Treasurer. On the left side was the blood red seal of the City of Toronto.

Frank smiled at the irony of the line "in every way a sterling young Canadian."

"We really have been accepted by the establishment," he laughed.

Steamer pulled up a chair and motioned for the others to do the same.

"I've told you boys how proud I am of you before, so I'm not going to reiterate the obvious," said Steamer. "You lads now have an opportunity to become the greatest hockey team in the world and I have every confidence you will accomplish just that."

There was a knock at the door and a hotel employee entered carrying a large cardboard box with *Canada* stenciled on the outside. Maxwell signed for the box, tipped the employee and placed the large carton on the floor in the middle of the room. Steamer tore away the packing tape and folded back the flaps. The contents were hidden by several thick layers of white tissue paper. The coach lifted out a yellow turtleneck sweater with CANADA in white stitched across a red maple leaf on a black background. The neck, cuffs and hemline were highlighted in black. He held it up for inspection and there was a gasp of admiration from every man in the room.

"This is a dream." Frank took the wool sweater from Maxwell and ran his hand across the white lettering.

"Put it on, Frankie," said Slim.

Frank pulled the turtleneck over his head and adjusted it to fit his broad shoulders. It was a perfect fit. The teammates inspected their captain. He cut a splendid figure in the new uniform. Frank's eyes watered and as he looked about the room he noted a similar emotion on every face. Coach Maxwell reached into the box and handed out jerseys to each player. They accepted them like communicants receiving Holy Communion.

"I wish Olive could see me now," said Slim, donning his jersey.

"Look at this!" Goodman dug further into the box. "There are pants and socks to match."

Maxwell sat down in a leather chair. He was as much overcome with sentiment as the team. He wondered how he would break his bad news to his players. He let them enjoy their moment of elation and delight a little longer.

"Gentlemen," he at last interjected. "I have some unwelcome news I must share with you."

The teammates looked from one to the other. What news could possibly spoil this occasion?

"Unfortunately, I won't be accompanying you to Antwerp," Steamer said. "I have business commitments in Calgary and as my lumber company is not well established, I can't afford to miss the meetings."

The room hushed.

Finally, Frank spoke. "There must be something you can do. You can't leave us now. You made us what we are. We can't go on alone."

Steamer sighed. "I didn't make you. I simply coaxed the best out of you and taught you to play as a team. You've always been champions.

You just needed a little guidance. And now I have nothing more to teach you—the rest is up to you."

Maxwell stood up and shook hands with each of the players. "My train leaves in an hour. Good luck and God bless."

"Who's going to be our manager?" asked Slim as Maxwell turned to leave.

"Billy Hewitt, the Toronto sports writer."

CHAPTER THIRTY-FOUR

"*T*his tub could use some extra ballast," complained Frank whose stomach heaved with every roll of the ship.

The Olympics were only weeks away and the Falcons did not have time to return to Winnipeg after their Allan Cup victory. Instead, they were hustled aboard a train for St. John where they embarked on the Canadian Pacific Railway steamer *Melita* for a seven day journey to Liverpool.

Frank and Konnie were in the ship's hold checking crates that contained their hockey equipment. The defenseman was concerned. One of the pine crates was missing.

"We've got a problem."

"I don't want to hear about it," said Frank, with a white face. He leaned against a bulkhead for support.

Konnie made a final search of the cargo.

"The crate containing our hockey sticks is missing."

Frank pulled himself upright.

"It can't be. The CPR had it listed on the bill of lading after we left harbor."

"It may have been listed but my guess is it's still on Pier 101 in St. John," said Konnie.

The boys climbed the stairs to the deck where the Falcons' staterooms were located. They banged on doors to rouse their teammates, most of whom swore and remained in their bunks.

"What's up?" Slim appeared with a towel covering his mouth.

"Our hockey sticks aren't on board," said Konnie. "It seems they were left in St. John."

"Jeezzus!" Slim vomited into his towel just as a frumpy, middle-aged woman in a gaudy frock approached.

The woman stopped and glowered at Slim.

"Did you just take the Lord's name in vain, young man?"

"Damn right," said Slim, "but I only do it on exceptional occasions."

The corpulent woman reached up and grabbed Slim by the ear.

"Do you know who I am young sir?" she demanded.

"No," said Slim.

"I'm Henrietta Muir Edwards of the Women's Christian Temperance Union and I do not abide swearing, vulgarity, smoking, or the consumption of alcohol in my presence."

At that moment, a slender, elderly man with a thick white beard, a bald pate, and a hand-rolled cigarette dangling from his lips came strolling along the hallway. He smelled of rum.

"Aye young mates," he said to the boys. "I see you've got yourselves in a mess of trouble with Henrietta Edwards, upholder of all that's sacred in this life."

He removed the cigarette from his lips, put his face as close as possible to Henrietta's, and blew smoke and rum fumes into her flaring nostrils.

"Let go of the boy's ear you overblown bag of Christian benevolence," he said. "You and your troop of puritans have already caused enough misery aboard this ship to make Davy Jones' locker preferable."

Henrietta did not let go of Slim's ear; she tightened her grip.

"How dare you speak to a Christian lady in such coarse terms you filthy little man. You'll live in everlasting perdition when you leave this earth."

The man pulled a mickey from the pocket of his overalls, taking a strong pull on the bottle.

"That may be," he replied, "but I prefer the devil's abode because Lucifer's not a self-righteous, judgmental, Bible-basher like you."

"Enough! I shall report you to the captain immediately."

She gave Slim's ear a final tug, then marched down the corridor.

"Tell Captain Jennings that Jake Sawyer, ship's carpenter, sends his regards."

Frank and Konnie looked at Sawyer with interest.

"Did you say you're a carpenter?" asked Frank.

"That's right, lad. Best damn wood butcher on the seven seas and not an ounce of conceit in me, though there's a tot of rum or two."

"Have you ever made a hockey stick Mr. Sawyer?" asked Frank.

Sawyer guffawed.

"I'm from Halifax, lad. We invented the game of hockey. Haven't ya heard of the Halifax Rules of Hockey? First official rule book ever published. As a matter of fact, I used to be a pretty good puck whacker myself. I once scored a goal..."

Frank politely interrupted. He had a feeling that Mr. Sawyer was prone to telling long-winded yarns.

"We happen to be in need of some hockey sticks. Do you think you could make at least 16 between now and our arrival at Liverpool?"

Sawyer scratched his stubble chin, contemplating.

"What do you need 'em for?"

"We're on our way to Antwerp to represent Canada at the Olympics."

"I'll be a coxswain's uncle!" exclaimed Sawyer. "I heard the Canadian Olympic hockey team was aboard. Never thought I'd meet 'em in person."

Sawyer held out his callused hand to the boys.

"This is a grand day for old Jake Sawyer. You lads follow me down to the workshop and we'll pick out the best lumber for your sticks."

Sawyer's workshop was in the bowels of the ship. It was equipped with a drill press, table saw, jointer and other machines the teammates didn't recognize. On a neatly organized work bench were carving chisels, hand planes, and drafting tools including French curves and compasses.

Sawyer led them to a corner of the spacious shop where piles of meticulously stickered wood were stored.

He pointed to a lift of lumber. "Here's what ya want for your sticks, lads."

Sawyer removed a piece from the pile and threw it to Konnie.

"Take a look down the edge of that plank, lad. You won't find a straighter piece of lumber between here and Nova Scotia."

Konnie examined the board. It was certainly straight and there were no knots.

"Why Nova Scotia?" he asked.

"Because you're holding Nova Scotia gold, the finest white ash grown in Canada. Indians made bows of it 'cause it's strong and springy. Just the properties you want in a first-rate hockey stick."

Frank and Slim, feeling better now the ship had stopped rolling, stepped forward and examined the plank of ash.

"Okay, Mr. Sawyer," said Frank. "You're hired. How much will the sticks cost?"

"They won't cost a plug of tobacco if you bring home the gold medal. Now get out of here, I've work to do."

CHAPTER THIRTY-FIVE

Antwerp, Belgium, April 1920

*F*rank was astonished that the 15th century Cathedral of Notre Dame near the Botanical Gardens was spared by the German forces that razed much of Antwerp with artillery during the war. The city was chosen as the site for the VII Olympiade because it suffered some of the worst destruction and casualties at the hands of the occupying Germany army. The Olympics stood for world peace. What better place than Antwerp to begin the healing process to world harmony?

The Falcons' bus stopped in front of the Queen's Hotel near Quai Van Dyck and a retinue of hotel employees scrambled out the front door to unload the team's equipment.

"Hold on," said Konnie. "There's one crate I'm not letting out of my sight. It's going to be kept in my room throughout the Olympics."

The Falcons and curious hotel employees gathered round Konnie as he pried open the crate's lid to examine the contents. There was a gasp of admiration from the men when the lid was thrown back. Inside were 16 exquisite ash hockey sticks. On each shaft the carpenter had carved the name of the owner in calligraphy: *Frank Fredrickson Esq.* was visible on a stick at the top of the pile.

"You Canadians should win the gold medal if only for the beauty of your sticks," laughed one porter.

"We're going to need more than those to beat the Americans," said manager Billy Hewitt approaching the group. He was followed by team president Hebbie Axford, club secretary Bill Fridfinnson, and trainer Gudmundur Sigurjonsson.

Hewitt ushered the teammates into the hotel, got them checked in, and called a team meeting in his room for 8 p.m. The boys were weary from their days of travel and were happy to get some food and rest before the conference with Hewitt.

Frank and Slim settled in their room and discussed Billy Hewitt.

"What do you think of this guy?" asked Slim. "He's a journalist not a coach."

Frank, who was hanging clothes in a spacious closet, took time to answer.

"The way I hear it," he said, "Hewitt knows more about hockey than any man in Canada. I don't think Steamer would leave us in the hands of a rank amateur."

Slim puffed his pillow and lay back on his bed.

"I guess we'll find out more about him at tonight's meeting."

———•◦•———

Billy Hewitt was a man of slight build. His dark hair was turning white at the temples and his hazel eyes had the discerning power of a man who has spent his life as a journalist. He saw and recorded the smallest details.

"Gentlemen," he said, standing to address the assembled teammates, "we have some matters to discuss before your game against Czechoslovakia tomorrow."

"First of all, you'll be playing the old style of seven-man hockey so coach Maxwell has instructed me to insert Woodman as rover."

The teammates hooted as Huck got to his feet and took a bow.

"Second," said Hewitt, "the ice surface here was designed for figure skating and ice dancing so it's about two-thirds the size of a Canadian rink. You're going to be bumping into each other if you don't play your positions at all times. And finally, I've spoken with officials of the International Ice Hockey Federation and they've agreed to adopt Canadian rules of play for the tournament. The only difference is you'll play two periods instead of three. Are there questions?"

"What makes you think you can manage this team? You're a journalist," said Slim.

"Steamer told me you boys are capable of managing yourselves," retorted Hewitt.

CHAPTER THIRTY-SIX

*T*he interior of Antwerp's Le Palais de Glace stadium was a shock to the Falcons. At ice level there were dining tables covered with white linen set with sterling silver flatware, crystal wine glasses, and tapered vases filled with flowers. At the north end a full orchestra played works by Vivaldi, Liszt, Tchaikovsky and Dvořák. German and Austrian composers were struck from the repertoire because of their countries' participation in the war.

Netting was hung around the rink to protect diners and musicians during hockey games. The boards, Frank noticed, were made of planks of irregular thickness which would make rebounds unpredictable. The goal nets were made of chicken wire bent around steel posts secured to the ice with short nails.

"Well, at least they painted the posts red," said Frank to Konnie.

Slim scanned the dining tables as the boys headed to the changing room.

"Folks sure have a short attention span here."

Billy Hewitt was waiting for them. He paced the room carrying a pad of yellow copy paper.

"It's about time you arrived. You've got less than 10 minutes to get dressed."

Hewitt consulted his sheaf of paper and summarized his notes.

"I scouted the Czechs this afternoon. They run on their skates, have weak shots, and don't play their positions. Go out there and beat them, but don't humiliate them."

Loud applause greeted the Falcons when they skated onto the ice. The people of Belgium were thankful to Canadians for liberating their war-torn country from the Germans.

The Czechs were already on the ice. They were dressed like soccer players with no upper body padding or shin guards and their sticks looked like curved branches with the bark removed with a hewing axe. Their skates were work boots with long straight blades screwed to the bottoms.

Frank won the face-off and passed the puck to Slim on right wing. He easily skated through the defenders and scored a goal on the first shot of the game.

At the end of the first half it was 10-0 Canada. By the middle of the second half, the Falcons had scored five more goals before Billy Hewitt signaled them to quit. Slim had seven markers, Frank four, Goodman two, Johannesson and Woodman one apiece.

Czechoslovaks Are Easy For Canadians
By Billy Hewitt (for the Free Press)

ANTWERP, BELGIUM, April 24 – By a score of 15 goals to nothing, the Falcons easily disposed of the Czechoslovak aggregation of puck chasers on Saturday, and won the right to compete in the semi-finals. The game witnessed the first appearance of the speedy Icelanders in an Olympic contest and their brilliant skating and exceptionally clever stick handling was a revelation to the crowd. The teamwork of the Canadian players against the stubborn but futile defense of their opponents evoked many rounds of applause from the spectators...

Canada plays the powerful American team tomorrow, April 25. The odds-makers are giving the Canadians a slight edge, but "this game is not a foregone conclusion," says Falcons' captain Frank Fredrickson. He says one thing is certain—the winner will take home the gold medal.

CHAPTER THIRTY-SEVEN

*B*elgium, indeed all of Europe, was in a frenzy over the game between the Canadians and the Americans. Huge sums were being wagered on the contest. The teams were so closely matched bookies were offering even odds on the outcome.

Bill Fridfinnson, the Falcons' secretary, seated comfortably in the lobby of the Queen's Hotel, was approached by an American lieutenant who wanted to bet on the Canada vs. U.S. match. The young Yank made such an outrageous wager that Fridfinnson thought the soldier was joking.

"My friends and I have 1,000 francs to bet on the Americans," said the well-groomed American officer.

"Make it 10,000 and I'll consider it," said Fridfinnson offhandedly.

"I'm not sure we can raise that much," said the soldier. "I'll have to speak to the lads in my unit."

The lieutenant promised to return with his answer as soon as possible and Fridfinnson thought nothing more of the matter.

A few hours later while Fridfinnson was eating lobster in the hotel's elegant dining room, the American lieutenant returned saying he could only scrape together 8,000 francs.

"It's 10,000 or nothing," said Fridfinnson, who still considered it a jest.

The American left saying he'd raise the 10,000 if he had to borrow a franc from every soldier in the U.S. army of occupation.

"What was that all about?" asked Hewitt. He sat down to have lunch with Fridfinnson.

"Just some crazy Yank who's pretending to wager outrageous sums on the outcome of tonight's game," said Fridfinnson with a dismissive wave of his hand.

Hewitt sat back in his padded armchair, lit a Dominican cheroot, poured himself a Premier Napoleon brandy and thought about the matter.

"You're not a gambling man are you, Bill?" he asked.

"Not really," replied Fridfinnson.

"So you think this crazy Yank is just pulling your leg?"

"Of course," said Fridfinnson.

Hewitt leaned forward, planting his elbows on the table.

"I've got some bad news. That soldier is dead serious and you've just got yourself into a mess of trouble."

Fridfinnson turned pale. He reached for the brandy, slopped a large measure into a water glass and downed most of it in a single swig.

"Perhaps he won't return," he said.

Hewitt puffed on his cheroot and sipped his brandy.

"If he does, we'd better be prepared to take his wager: there's nothing more despicable than a man who refuses to cover a bet."

Twenty minutes later, the American appeared at their table with a despondent look on his face.

"I could only scrounge up 8,000 francs," he said.

The two Canadians looked at each other with some relief.

"We'd be honored to accept." Fridfinnson took another gulp of brandy as he shook the soldier's hand.

CHAPTER THIRTY-EIGHT

*E*ither Canada or America would win the world's first gold hockey medal ever presented at the Olympic Games. The crème de la crème of European society had spent more money to attend the game than an ordinary man could earn in a year. Lesser dignitaries had squandered their fortunes to purchase scalped tickets; the Palais de Glace was, after all, the place to be seen and hockey fever had swept Europe. Men and women who couldn't afford admission presented themselves to the Falcons as dukes and duchesses, offering to carry skates or hockey sticks into the arena in exchange for an opportunity to see the game first-hand. Each Falcon had a dozen porters of noble lineage escort him into the rink.

"I didn't realize that European royalty could be so kind and accommodating," said Slim, bowing to the Prince of Milano, who carried Slim's hockey stick.

Frank and the rest of the teammates howled.

"For a Bolshie, you certainly are impressed by the upper classes," said Mike.

"Especially the phony ones," added Friddy.

Slim was offended. "What do you mean phony? The prince told me all about his castle in Italy and his father the king."

He turned to the prince for confirmation. The man handed Slim the hockey stick and disappeared among the crowd inside the arena.

Billy Hewitt greeted the Falcons as they entered the changing room. The walls were hung with brocade woven with gold and silver designs and the benches, if they could be called benches, were covered with purple velvet.

"I'm not going to say much," said Hewitt. "We all know what this game means. The word on the Americans is they'll use their weight advantage to body check hard. Don't let them throw you off your game and don't let them provoke you into unnecessary penalties. Good luck."

Hewitt left the room and made his way to the press box where he would cover the match for the Canadian press.

The teammates hid their nerves by paying attention to details: adjusting shin and shoulder pads; checking for broken reinforcement sticks in their gloves; lacing and unlacing skates until the correct tightness was achieved; and, most importantly, wrapping the right amount of tape around the blades of their sticks. Too little and the blade could be snapped from the shaft, too much and the stick became an unwieldy club.

Huck broke the tense quiet.

"Well, look at us. A Brit and seven Goolies off to do battle for the greatest hockey prize in history. Who'd have believed it?"

"Consider yourself a very lucky Brit to be in the company of such an august and talented group of Goolies," said Bobby.

"I do," said Huck. "And no matter what happens, win or lose, I'll never forget this experience or my friendship with you lads."

A man with a French accent knocked on the door.

"It is time to commence the competition."

The Falcons left the dressing-room led by Frank. Slim tapped his friend on the shoulder.

"Frankie, we forgot to touch the amulet for luck."

"We'll do it at half time," said Frank, whose hands shook.

There was an explosion of applause when the Canadians skated onto the ice. Moments later, there was an equal burst of enthusiasm when the Americans, led by captain Francis Moose Goheen, entered the rink. Both North American teams were admired by the Europeans for their exceptional hockey skills and their countries' roles in driving the Huns out of Belgium. The orchestra played the national anthems of both countries. Billy Hewitt, watching from the press booth, thought the Falcons looked tight and nervous in comparison to the Americans.

The face-off was between Frank and Joe McCormick. The big American center was an expatriate Canadian who'd learned his hockey in Quebec. He had two inches and 20 pounds on Frank. When the puck was dropped, he shoved Frank out of the way, scooped up the puck, and lugged it into the Falcons' end. McCormick's shot was a burner that nearly knocked Wally off his feet when it hit him in the chest. The rebound was grabbed by right-winger Tony Conroy. Conroy ripped a shot that Wally caught with his glove and held for a face-off in the Falcons' scoring zone.

Joe McCormick won the face-off cleanly from Frank, sliding the disc back to the rover, Moose Goheen. The husky player began a take-all rush that sent Falcon defenders spinning across the ice like tops. At the last moment Bobby jumped on the big man's shoulders, slowing him enough for Konnie to get into position to block his shot. Some members of the crowd demanded Bobby get a penalty, while others applauded his effort. The referee, a Frenchman, Alfred de Rauch, allowed play to continue. The blocked shot was picked up by left-winger Herb Drury, another expatriate Canadian, who fired a high shot that hit the crossbar and bounced into the netting that surrounded the lower part of the Ice Palace.

Yet another face-off was held in the Falcons' zone. Frank again lost the draw and McCormick flipped the puck back to defenseman Ed Fitzgerald. Fitzgerald fired a low shot that was almost deflected into the Falcons' net by McCormick. The rebound was pounced on by Gerry Geran. He had muscled into the slot from his defense position. His blast clipped Wally on the cheekbone, caroming into the corner of the rink where Konnie and Conroy fought for possession. Conroy rammed his shoulder into Konnie's backbone forcing him to lose control of the puck. The enraged Falcons' defenseman took a wild swing with his stick which just missed his opponent's head.

The referee rang his bell to stop play. He called both teams to center ice where he explained the term "unsportsmanlike conduct."

"If it should happen again, the player will receive a major penalty," he said, looking at Konnie.

Before play resumed, Frank had the teammates gather around Wally's net.

"We've got to settle down here. They're killing us with their body checks," Frank said.

"There isn't enough room on this sheet for our style of play. It's impossible to get a clean, fast break without being slammed to the ice," said Mike.

"I know," said Frank. "But we have to find a way to use our speed and our stick handling skills otherwise they're going to take us apart. So far Wally has kept us in the game, but we can't depend on him forever. Let's try two-man rushes to see if we can get some skating room."

The bell rang to resume play. The face-off was in the Falcons' end to the left of Wally. Frank won the draw and began a corkscrew rush up the ice with Mike matching him stride for stride. As Frank crossed center ice, Moose Goheen lined him up for a crushing check that the Falcons' center took head on, still managing to slide the puck to Mike. The left-winger sprinted into the American's zone where he was tied up by the defenseman Geran. Mike managed a weak shot on goal easily deflected by the Canadian-trained goaltender, Ray Bonney. The loose puck was picked up by McCormick who steamed down center ice with Conroy on one side and Drury on the other. The threesome converged on the Falcons' citadel, splitting the defense. McCormick passed to Drury. He had a wide open net and would have scored if not for a tremendous back checking effort by Goodman. He caught Drury from behind, preventing a dangerous shot on goal. Slim found the loose puck but was smashed into the boards by Goheen before he could start a rush. The Americans continued to dominate the play with punishing checks as the bell rang to end the first period.

The Falcons limped into their dressing room each nursing bruises or cuts inflicted by the brutal play of the Americans. Wally's cheek required a couple of stitches by trainer Sigurjonsson. The boys sat on the plush benches with their heads down. To have come this far only to be denied a gold medal by a team of thugs seemed unfair. Frank could feel the great Olympic dream slipping from his grasp.

CHAPTER THIRTY-EIGHT

Huck could see the discouragement on his captain's face and spoke up.

"Do you remember the fight we had on the Assiniboine River all those years ago?"

"Sure," said Frank. "How could I forget?"

"I had the advantage because I knew how to use my body," said Huck.

"You certainly did," recalled Frank, rubbing his jaw.

"And yet no matter how many times I knocked you down, you kept getting up."

"I guess that's what Icelanders are all about," said Frank. "We just don't know when to quit."

"Exactly," said Huck. "I feared and respected you that day because I knew you would never quit, no matter how many times I belted you."

Frank stared at his Wasp friend.

"I get your point," Frank said to Huck. "The verb 'to quit' is not in the Goolie vocabulary."

Frank got to his feet and addressed his teammates. "We still have 20 minutes of hockey left. Let's show the Americans that Goolies never give up, no matter how tough the going gets."

He removed the amulet from inside his jersey. The teammates gathered round to touch the charm. "What's our dream!" bellowed Frank.

Everyone yelled back, "To become the greatest, most respected, most renowned, most beloved team of hockey players in the world."

CHAPTER THIRTY-NINE

The Falcons skated a fast warm-up lap around the rink. Billy Hewitt was astonished at the difference in their demeanor from the opening period. Their body language relayed the confidence and the indomitable spirit that was the hallmark of their Viking ancestors.

"What did you say to your team between periods, Billy?" asked an American reporter, sitting beside Hewitt in the press box.

"I didn't say anything. There wasn't time for me to get to the dressing room and back before the second period."

"Well someone sure put some Nordic pride and a shot of maple syrup in their tanks," said the American.

Frank won the face-off, passing the puck to Slim. He took a vicious hit from Drury but managed to keep control of the disc. He carried it into the American corner where Geran rammed him into the boards. Geran was taken out by Woodman, moving up from his rover position to help his winger. Slim centered the disc to Frank. He rifled a shot at Bonney from directly in front of the net. The powerful drive hit the U.S. goalie on the chest, almost knocking him into the net. The rebound came to Frank. He was leveled by Goheen before he could unleash a second shot. Goodman snatched the disc, flipping a backhand over Bonney's shoulder that hit the crossbar. McCormick grabbed the puck and began a rush up the ice, only to be caught from behind by Goodman. The puck bounced across the ice to Konnie. The defenseman bulled his way down the ice knocking American players off their feet, but eventually was dragged to the ice by Goheen. The referee rang his bell to stop play and Goheen was assessed a major penalty, giving the Falcons a man advantage and room to maneuver on the small sheet of ice.

McCormick won the face-off in the American zone and cleared the puck down the ice. Benson dug it out of his own corner and began a rush with Frank at center and Mike on left wing. Benson was hammered by Drury, but managed to flip the puck to Frank. Faking a pass to Mike, Fredrickson charged straight at the American net, unleashing a blistering shot that was kicked out by Bonney. The rebound came straight back to the Falcons' center. Taking a rib-cracking check from McCormick, Frank banged the puck home between Bonney's legs.

A large contingent of British soldiers raised a Falcon banner and chanted.

"Canada, Canada, Canada!"

European spectators, who'd never witnessed such a fast-paced sport, stood on their seats and applauded the efforts of both teams.

"They must have motors in their skates," one member of the Swedish Olympic team commented to a friend.

In the press booth, Hewitt said, "Get this on the wire right away. 'Fredrickson has scored for Canada at 11 minutes of the second period.'"

He turned to Fridfinnson who sat beside him. "How shall we spend our 8,000 francs?"

"It's not over yet," said the Falcons' secretary, biting his nails for the first time in his life.

The face-off was at center ice. When the puck was dropped, Frank and McCormick became entangled as they battled for the puck. McCormick broke away with the disc and Frank tripped him with his stick. The bell rang to stop play. Frank was given a minor penalty.

The Americans took advantage by blitzing the Falcons' citadel. Both defensemen and the rover pinched into the scoring zone taking shot after shot at Wally. The beleaguered goalie made a dozen saves in a row, the most spectacular an outstretched glove stop that broke his finger but prevented a sure goal. The onslaught continued with the Americans buzzing around the goal like warplanes firing at will. The pressure was relieved by Huck. He finally managed to flip the disc high in the air, placing it in the American end. Fitzgerald took control. He corkscrewed up the ice maneuvering through the entire Canadian team. His high shot caromed off Bobby's elbow and hit the goal post. The loose puck was stopped by Konnie just before it crossed the goal line.

In the press box, Hewitt and Fridfinnson looked at each other.

"There is a God," said Hewitt.

"Of course there is." Fridfinnson tore a large piece of nail from his thumb.

His penalty over, Frank leaped onto the ice just in time to stop McCormick from winding up for yet another rush on the Falcons' net. Slim picked up the loose disc only to be flattened by Conroy. He broke into the Falcon scoring zone, releasing a bullet at Wally. The rebound was scooped up by Mike in full flight. He blazed down the left wing, split the defense and ripped a shot at Bonney that cracked his goalie stick. The American net-minder swept the disc to Geran in the corner. Slim skated in, ramming Geran into the boards and centering the puck to Frank in front of the net. Goheen tried to drag Frank to the ground with his stick, but the Falcons' center wrestled the American to the ice instead. Frank fired a wicked wrist shot that just missed the right side of the net. Mike moved behind the American citadel, ploughed Fitzgerald into the boards, then passed the puck to Frank. He rifled another shot that was caught at the last second by Bonney. Frank put his shoulder into Bonney's chest, knocking him inside the net. The bell rang and the Falcons' center was given a major penalty.

"Damn," said Hewitt. "What a thing to happen just when we were gaining the momentum."

Fridfinnson said nothing. He was running out of fingernails to chew.

With Canada's star in the penalty box, the Americans prepared to press hard. If there was an opportunity to win the game, this was it.

Slim took the face-off, beat McCormick cleanly, and covered the length of the ice in a few long strides. He dropped the puck for Mike who ragged the disc into the American's zone, then carried it back toward center ice, weaving around his opponents with finesse. His exhibition of speed and stick handling was applauded by the crowd. The frustrated U.S. team chased the wily speed skater up and down the ice until he was finally knocked to the ice by McCormick at center. Huck checked McCormick and threw the puck across the ice to Slim. The right-winger put on a stick handling show of his own that also earned the respect of the fans. The momentum remained with the Canadians as they continued to kill Frank's penalty.

Fredrickson's penalty finally ended, but with five minutes to play it was still anyone's match. Frank won a face-off in his own end and passed the puck to Slim. Avoiding a check by Goheen, Slim passed the puck to Konnie. The defenseman fought mightily to get the disc to Mike. The speedster rushed down the left wing and passed the puck across ice to Slim on right wing. Slim took a hit from Goheen and dropped the disc back to Konnie. He began a take-all rush up the ice. The big defenseman was carrying Goheen and Drury on his shoulders when he blasted a shot from 20 feet out that beat Bonney.

"Johannesson has scored with four minutes left in the game! Get that on the wire!" screamed Hewitt on his feet.

A small group of Canadian supporters applauded wildly. When Frank looked up to see who the patriots in the crowd were, he was amazed to spot Laycock, Solmundson, and Levine, as well as Haldora and Minnie waving to him from expensive seats near center ice.

"Well I'll be damned," he said to himself, waving back. "I wonder if Fat Mac MacPherson appreciates irony."

The Falcons continued to take the game to the Americans, refusing to protect their lead by playing defensively. When the bell rang to signal the end of the game, the Falcons swarmed around Wally, hefted him off the ground and skated around the rink, holding their goalie aloft. The crowd in the Ice Palace stood on its feet and cheered the Canadian victory. Paul Levine of Laycock & Co. jumped over the boards and ran after the Falcons as they took their victory lap. Haldora and Minnie were in tears. Barring a miracle victory by the Swedes over the Falcons in the final match of the tournament, the improbable team from Winnipeg would soon be crowned hockey champions of the world.

"Do Vikings ever give up?" Laycock asked of Solmundson.

"Did Leif Ericson cross the Atlantic in a 75-foot boat?" replied Solmundson.

CHAPTER FORTY

*T*he Swedes played hockey like the English played rugby. No holds barred. Equipment such as shin and elbow pads was considered sissy stuff. As a result, the Swedish hockey team sustained more injuries during the Olympics than any other entrant.

Despite the Nordic team's rugged approach to the game, bookmakers were offering 1,000 to one odds against the Swedish puck whackers beating Canada in the Olympic gold medal final. Some fans from Sweden, however, remained optimistic. Their team had easily defeated Belgium 8-0 and France 4-0 on the Swedes' march to the gold final against Canada. A few diehard supporters were convinced the Swedish team could perform the impossible and beat the Canadians.

There was a good rapport between the Canadians and the Swedes because the Falcons' trainer, Gudmundur Sigurjonsson, had ministered to the entire Swedish Olympic hockey team, suturing cuts and setting broken bones many times. The Falcon teammates also had taken a liking to the Swedes. During practices the Canadians would coach the Swedes from the sidelines, teaching them the fine points of passing and stick handling a hockey puck. In their country, the Swedes played a game called bandy on a sheet of ice the size of a soccer field. They wore speed skates and carried a short stick to bat a ball into a large net. The Swedes were proficient skaters, but their long, flat-bladed skates prevented them from stopping and starting quickly or from maneuvering deftly around opponents. After their 8-0 win over Belgium, Frank congratulated the Swedes saying: "Well done, but it was not ice hockey!"

The evening of the gold medal game the Ice Palace was sold out. European spectators were dumbfounded by the Canadians' skating skills, especially those of Mike Goodman who had demonstrated barrel jumping and trick skating at a special performance that afternoon.

Just before the opening face-off, Frank coached the Swedish center on techniques for winning the draw as soon as the puck was dropped. He allowed the center, Hansjacob Mattsson, to win the face-off and carry the rubber into the Falcon zone. Mattsson was poke checked by Fridfinnson, playing rover in place of Woodman. Benson picked up the puck and began one of his famous corkscrew rushes down the ice. He passed the disc to Halderson. Using his deceptive speed, the right-winger beat defenseman Einar Lindqvist and scored the first goal at the one-minute mark. The Falcons scored two more markers in quick succession, then slowed down the game. Goodman ragged the puck around the ice, showing off his skating skills. Finally, he unleashed a blast at Swedish goalie, Seth Howander. The puck caught the net-minder in the forehead. The gash required stitches and a time out was called. While Sigurjonsson patched up the Swedish net-minder, the Falcons gathered round Wally.

"I like these Swedes," said Frank. "If they had the right skates, they could be contenders."

"Why don't we let them score," said Wally. "At least they can return home with something to boast about."

It was agreed that after the face-off the Falcons would suddenly become confused, trip over each other, and allow the Swedes a breakaway.

Frank purposely lost the draw, allowing Mattsson to pass the puck to rover Einar Svensson. The rover picked his way slowly around the Falcons' defenders who fell to the ice at his approach. When the Swede skated awkwardly into the scoring zone, Bobby and Konnie ran into each other leaving Svensson a clear shot on goal. Wally fell to his knees pretending to be shocked by the power of the shot and the puck bounced off his skate into the net.

Shrill whistles greeted the miraculous goal. The Swedes pounded each other on the back and hugged Svensson. He had been elevated to the level of national hero.

The Falcons led 5-1 after the first period. The game ended 12-1 with Frank accounting for seven goals; the rest were divided among Slim, Mike, Bobby and Friddy. When the final bell rang, the teammates swarmed around Frank, then collapsed in a heap at center ice, congratulating each other on their extraordinary world championship triumph.

"Goolies never quit!" yelled Frank at the roaring spectators. The fans continued to cheer after the Falcons left the ice.

At the medal presentation ceremony, the teammates stood on stage. They held their gold medals proudly above their heads. Frank spotted his friends from Laycock & Co. in the crowd and called to them to join the team, but security police halted the group. Frank jumped from the podium and pushed through the police. He embraced each of his friends.

"Well done Frank!" said Sam Laycock. "You've lived up to our great expectations."

"From one Goolie to another, congratulations Frank!" exclaimed Halson Solmundson.

"A champion of the world," said Paul Levine. "Wait till I write my friends in the old country and tell them about this."

Haldora and Minnie kissed Frank until his face was covered in red lipstick.

"I knew you were something special the first time I saw you, sweetie," said Minnie.

The security men gave way when they realized the captain of the Canadian team wished to lead Sam Laycock and his colleagues on to the podium to share the Olympic victory.

The Canadian flag was raised and a cheering mob that filled the Ice Palace saluted the indomitable team from Winnipeg.

It was a bittersweet moment for Frank. He felt elated and yet slightly disappointed. He had realized his dream, but he knew this flash of glory would fade like an imploding star. What would be next?

CHAPTER FORTY-ONE

*T*he teammates were relaxing in the rotunda of the Queen's Hotel awaiting the arrival of a bus that would take them to Antwerp harbor from where they would travel to Paris for a reception hosted by the Commissioner of the Saar Valley, Robert Waugh, a former Winnipegger. The players smoked the first cigarettes and sipped the first beer they had tasted since the strict Steamer Maxwell had become their coach almost a year ago.

The world champions were approached by Einar Svensson, the rover who had scored the Swedish team's only goal against the Canadians. He was accompanied by the Falcons' trainer, Gudmundur Sigurjonsson

"Einar wants to buy your skates," the trainer said to Mike.

"Whatever for?" asked Mike.

"He thinks they have some sort of miniature motors in them to make you skate so fast."

The teammates did not burst into laughter in deference to Einar's feelings. They looked at Mike with intense smiles on their faces.

"How much is he willing to pay?" asked Mike.

"One hundred Canadian dollars," said the trainer.

The teammates were dumbfounded.

"Sell them Mike," said Friddy. "We're on our way to the City of Light. We could use that money."

Mike turned to the trainer for advice.

"Have you told him they're just ordinary skates?" he asked.

"Many times. But he won't believe me. It will hurt his feelings if you turn him down."

Mike looked at Einar who reached into his pocket and dug out a roll of Canadian bills. He offered them to Mike.

"Well, I certainly wouldn't want to hurt his feelings." Mike rummaged through his equipment bag for his skates and handed them to Einar.

The Swede held the skates as if they were Olympic gold medals. He lifted the tongues, searching inside the boots for the magic engines. Then he examined the blades and the tubes.

"Ah," he said, pointing to the tubes. "Engines here!" The Swede shook hands with Mike, delighted with his purchase.

The team bus pulled to a stop in front of the hotel. "Now to conquer Paris," said Mike. He wore his gold medal around his neck, refusing to take it off day or night.

CHAPTER FORTY-TWO

*F*easted and feted, the weary Falcons were glad to be on their way home after Paris, Montreal and Toronto. The boys spent most of their time on the train from Toronto to Winnipeg in their bunks catching up on some needed sleep. At mealtimes they chatted about their Olympic victory.

"I suppose they've already forgotten us in Winnipeg," said Slim.

It was May 22, almost seven weeks to the day since they had won the Allan Cup, when their train pulled into the CPR station at Main and Higgins. Much to the teammates' surprise a crowd was gathered at the platform. Charles Gray, the mayor of Winnipeg, climbed on board, shook the hand of each Falcon reverently, and handed out the finest Cuban cigars.

"Welcome home, gentlemen. What a splendid job! We've prepared a little homecoming ceremony for our conquering heroes." Behind Gray was Steamer Maxwell who thumped each player on the back.

Gray led the Falcons off the train where a crowd of thousands greeted them with a thunderous ovation. A half-day holiday had been declared for the celebration. The boys were ushered into a Cadillac open touring car that drove slowly down Main Street lined with jubilant fans who held up banners: "Welcome home World Champions" and "Winnipeg Loves the Falcons."

"I guess they haven't forgotten us," said Slim as the car turned onto Portage Avenue, jammed one either side with well-wishers calling "Hello, Slim," or "Atta boy, Wally," or "Great work, Steamer."

Slim jumped out of the car and became lost in the mass that swarmed Portage Avenue.

"Where the hell has he gone?" demanded Steamer.

"He's looking for his Juliet," said Frank.

Near the Eaton's building at the back of the crowd, Frank spotted Fat Mac Jr. standing alone. He looked so forsaken that Frank involuntarily waved to him. The young bully responded by spitting on the ground, then turned his back and disappeared into the shadows of Donald Street.

The parade ended at the Wesley College quadrangle where Mayor Gray ushered the Falcons onto a raised platform with a backdrop: "Welcome Home Olympic Champions." On a table festooned with cloth maple leaves were a dozen walnut boxes with the Olympic symbol of five interlacing rings carved into the lids. Mayor Gray removed a gold pocket watch from one of the boxes and held it up for the crowd to see. Inscribed on the watch were the words: *Congratulations to the Winnipeg Falcons on the advent of their gold medal victory at the VII Olympiade, Antwerp, Belgium, A.D. 1920.*

Each teammate was called forward to receive his watch from Mayor Gray. Slim's name was called and there was an embarrassing silence when the right-winger didn't appear. The mayor cleared his throat and tried once more.

"I'm here," yelled Slim, whose tall figure was visible in the middle of the horde. He was dragging a young woman behind him. "This is Olive McKay, the girl I'm going to marry," said Slim proudly.

"Well, that's a great piece of news!" Billy Finlay was covering the event for the Free Press.

Just then, Frank spotted Bea in the crowd.

"Come join us!" he called to the young woman.

Frank lifted Bea on the stage and gave her a hug, much to the delight of the onlookers.

"Give the lady a kiss, son," encouraged Jon Fredrickson, standing in the front row with his wife and Frank's brother, Jonas.

The delirious mob began to chant: "Kiss, kiss, kiss."

Frank took Bea in his arms and gave her a long, lingering kiss.

The next morning Frank opened the newspaper and smiled when he read the bold headline on the front page:

The Team Nobody Wanted Has Become
The Team Everybody Loves

ABOUT THE AUTHOR

David Square grew up in Winnipeg where he played shinny on outdoor rinks at River Heights Community Centre. He graduated from the University of Manitoba with a degree in English.

When Falcons Fly is Square's fourth book. He is the author of *The Veneering Book, The Manitoba Medical Service Foundation: 35 Years of Promoting Health Care in Manitoba,* and the e-book, *Hell's Elongated Bells.*

In 1976, he and his wife Penny completed a log house near Tyndall, Manitoba where they live today. Their daughter Bryn began figure skating on a backyard rink.

They earned their living for many years as one-of-a-kind furniture makers. One of their pieces was presented to Queen Elizabeth II by the Government of Manitoba.